Sweet on the Cowboy

Sweet on the Cowboy

The Draegers of Last Stand, Texas Romance

Sasha Summers

TULE
PUBLISHING

Dedication

To Jane Porter and her incredible spirit and inspiration
Thank you for letting me write cowboys for Tule!

Chapter One

L AM ROLLED HIS head, stretching muscles knotted from long hours of work and stress. His boots echoed off the polished wood floor leading to the kitchen. No need to tiptoe. Besides he and Jax, it was his mother and Marta. His mother had started taking sleeping pills after his father's passing—said she couldn't sleep without him "sawing logs" beside her—and Marta's room was at the other end of the house.

The whereabouts of his siblings? Not home and not his problem. They were adults, when they chose to act like it. According to his sister, Tabitha, he was the only Draeger who didn't have a social life. But all her poking and prodding and teasing about going out, having fun—even finding a hobby—sounded like work. And, dammit, he was already doing that from sun up to sun down running the ranch. Not that he minded too much. He loved this land, his home, with every fiber of his being. As far as he was concerned, there was nothing prettier than a sunrise or a sunset in the Texas Hill Country.

Jax's ears perked up and he whimpered once, earning Lam's attention.

"What's up?" he asked his shadow. Jax might be a working Australian Cattle Dog, but he was Lam's favorite companion. Maybe it was wrong to prefer a four-legged companion, but Jax was just about the only living thing that didn't expect him to shoulder their burdens, fix their problems, or need or want something from him. Except food, of course. Jax was fond of his chow. And Lam appreciated that.

Jax cocked his ears and whimpered again.

"We've been over this." Lam bent, rubbing a hand along Jax's head and neck. "I still don't speak dog."

If it was possible, Lam would swear Jax rolled his eyes at him. And this wasn't the first time either. Jax's devotion might be unwavering, but that didn't mean the dog found him amusing. Not in the least.

"Hungry?" He nodded. "Me too." Marta would have something waiting in the kitchen—for both of them. The highlight of his day. Maybe his sister was right. A hobby might be in order. Preferably a hobby that wouldn't require him to drive twenty minutes into town.

He stood, coming face-to-face with a framed photo of his father. Joseph Draeger. He wasn't smiling. He hadn't believed in smiling for photos. Not that he'd been much for smiling when there wasn't a camera involved either. His father had been a no-nonsense man with high expectations, unyielding principals, and was the keeper of long-standing tradition—no matter how archaic. In the four months since his father's death, Lam had been the one to take on the monumental task of managing the family ranch. In that short time, he'd come to respect his father's devotion to the ranch more than ever. And he resented the secrets his father had put on Lam to sort out now that he was gone. Secrets that included sending money to a woman in Arizona. Lam's stomach twisted.

Jax pawed at his calf.

"Yeah, yeah." He sighed, straightening the corner of the photo. "It's not right to talk ill of the dead. Or think it." His gaze swept over the wall covered with Draegers past and present.

His family was made up of hardworking, resourceful, and tough folk. Their word was their oath and their family always, *always*, came first. He cast another glance at his father. At least most of the time. Nothing like taking over the family finances to realize things weren't as no-nonsense as his father had led them all to believe. His fine, upstanding father had secrets, and Lam was left to sort those out, too.

Like always, the picture of Grant caught his eye. His boy's too-big cowboy hat and snaggle-toothed grin always lit up his world—before shredding his heart. He touched the picture, traced the curve of his son's smile, and fought to keep the grief at bay.

Jax nudged him with his nose.

He tore his gaze from Grant's picture, forcing himself to walk on. "I'm going." His stomach growled. "Let's go."

Marta had been spoiling him with her evening snacks since he was a boy. She was one of the few staples on the ranch and his life—one he truly valued now. From her willingness to listen and deliver useful matter-of-fact life lessons, to her incredible soul-soothing cooking. Blood or not, he'd always considered the woman family, and, so far, she was one of the few people who'd yet to get under his skin.

After today, he could use some frank talk and comfort

food. And, since the peaches were ripe, Marta would have made the most of the peach crop from his grandmother's orchard. His stomach grumbled as he imagined her still-warm bread with fresh peach butter. Walnut peach cookies. Peach and pecan tarts. Shortbread. Pies of every variety. It was a good damn thing he worked hard all day, or he'd be getting downright soft in the middle.

If he was lucky, she'd have coffee, too. He had paper-work that wouldn't wait, and a cup of steaming black coffee was the only way he'd keep his eyes open.

The not-so-soft strains of music reached him. Big band music? Marta didn't listen to anything but gospel music—mostly hymns sung by choirs. This was nothing like it. Horns, drums, and a toe-thumping rhythm. Definitely not Marta's style. The closer he got to the kitchen, the more curious he became. He pushed the hand-carved wooden door wide and paused, his curiosity morphing into confusion.

Who the hell was the woman making a mess in his kitch-en? Where was Marta? What was going on?

Irritation kicked in. He wasn't a fan of surprises. Especially ones that disrupted his routine. He'd had enough of that since his father's recent passing. And now this? Whatever this was?

With a whisk in one hand, the woman swayed back and forth on her polka-dotted sock-covered feet to the beat of the music. Her skirt, bright blue with pinstripes, hugged curvy hips and revealed shapely calves. Piles of copper curls were pinned on top of her head. And…was she wearing a tiara?

He scrubbed a hand over his face and shook his head. Maybe he'd fallen asleep at his desk again? This was a dream.

Possibly the strangest dream he'd ever had.

Jax trotted across the stone floor, the click of his nails masked by the blare of horns, to sniff at two little girls asleep on a mountain of pink pillows and fuzzy blankets beneath the long wooden kitchen table. Little girls. Asleep. Under his kitchen table.

They were wearing sparkly wings.

Because, why not? He opened his mouth, stared back at the woman, and waited.

She was too caught up in what she was doing to realize she had an audience.

The real question, besides the dozen obvious questions scrolling through his brain, was: how could the girls sleep through the music blaring from Marta's ancient radio? Which brought him back to, "Where is Marta?"

Whether he'd meant to ask his last question out loud was irrelevant. He had. Barked it, was more like it. Hard and sharp and loud.

The woman spun so sharply, her tiara wobbled, and a bit of whatever she was whisking dribbled to the floor with a splat. Brown eyes widened, and she shot a glance toward the sleeping girls before she said, "Shhh! You'll wake them."

Which was not the response he'd expected. Was she serious? "Excuse me?"

With her whisk, she pointed at the sleeping girls.

"Marta?" he repeated, softer. Wait, a minute... He was beyond irritated now.

"She's sleeping." Those brown eyes darted toward the clock, widened, then returned to him. She turned the radio down. "I hadn't realized it was so late."

It was almost eleven. Marta was up before dawn to have breakfast for the crew—she needed her sleep. But that didn't explain who this woman was, why she was here, or what the hell was going on. He cleared his throat and did his best not to bark this time. "And you are?"

She swiped at her cheek with the back of her hand, leaving a streak of flour. No, sugar. Her cheek glistened. "Gwen?"

Was that a question? How was he supposed to know who she was? He frowned.

"And *you* are?" Her tone was sharp. Wait. She was asking him questions, now? *She* was upset?

His frown grew. Hands on his hips, eyebrow raised, he bit out, "Lambert Draeger." He was tired and frustrated and hungry.

Her eyes went owl-like, round and startled. "Oh. You are? Lam… You're—"

"The owner of this ranch. And this kitchen. And the bowl and the whisk you're using? Yeah. That's mine." Watching the red streak across her cheeks was oddly satisfying. "But I have no idea who you are or why you're in my kitchen. And, considering the hour, I'd like an explanation. Quick like."

"I'm cooking." Her dismayed gaze swept over the stack of bowls, marble countertop covered in flour, and general mess.

He waited for the rest. Nothing. "I can see that much," he prompted.

"It's an amazing kitchen. Completely different." She stared around the room with a sort of awe. "Guess time got away from me."

He didn't know what to make of that. Any of this, to be honest. Something about the sincere tenderness on her face cooled his irritation—somewhat. And piqued his curiosity. She was an odd duck. "You're not some strange sort of burglar who breaks into places to mess up their kitchen, are you?" He nodded at the sleeping girls. "And those are your accomplices?"

Her smile was quick. And devastating. "No. Of course not."

He swallowed, all too aware of the dimple in her cheek. Odd. And an eyeful. A mighty pleasing eyeful. "That's a relief." He crossed, running a finger through the flour covering the marble countertop...and discovering a plate piled high with delectable-looking pastries. "I'll eat one of those, and you can answer the rest of my questions. You know, give me a reason not to call the sheriff."

"The sheriff?" she squeaked.

He bit into the flaky light pastry and moaned. "Mmm." He chewed, the flavors—butter and cream cheese and peach and sugar—melting on his tongue. "Did you make these?"

"Maybe." Her brown eyes narrowed. "Maybe I'm some sort of burglar who breaks into places, messes up kitchens, and bakes pastries." She paused. "Poisoned pastries."

He shot her a look. "Honestly?" He finished off one and reached for another. "I can think of worse ways to go. These are incredible." He bit into the fresh pastry. "Now, start talking."

"What? You don't know who I am? No, I guess not. I'm Marta's daughter." She blew one of the copper curls from her face. "I'm staying for a while. Letting her have a vacation while I fill in here in the kitchen."

He paused midchew. What the hell was she talking about? "Excuse me?" The rest of her delivery sunk in. *This* was Marta's globe-trotting daughter? The one who hadn't bothered to visit her for the last five years? The one he'd found Marta crying into her apron over more times than he could count? She shows up here and messes up his kitchen, and he's just supposed to smile and nod and be okay with it? "You said you're filling in for her?"

She nodded. "Temporarily. She wanted to spend time with her granddaughters. I am a chef—"

"Who approved this?" He was barking again. But, dammit, Marta was his rock, his sounding board. And it would be nice if he had control of one small part of his life, just once.

A crinkle developed between Gwen's brows. "Approved?"

"I'll repeat myself. My kitchen. My house. My employees." He set the rest of his pastry on the counter. "I do the hiring and firing around here."

She was all owl-eyed again. "But..."

"Mrs...?"

"*Miss* Hobbs." She stiffened somewhat, the tilt of her head almost defiant. "Gwendolyn Hobbs."

He'd struck a nerve. It was hard to miss the emphasis on *Miss*. No husband then. Not that it mattered. This had nothing to do with her and everything to do with...him. Life. Control. Being left in charge of the ranch hadn't been a complete surprise—he'd been the only one who hadn't found some other vocation to occupy himself. But his father's death had determined his future, without his input or approval or confirmation. Some days, the complete and utter lack of control he had over every facet of his life was overwhelming. He rubbed a hand over his face again, swallowing against the frustration and anger rising up. "I don't know you, Miss Hobbs."

"You do, actually," she argued. "I lived here until I was twelve. After that, I went to stay with my father. Not that you'd remember that. You were already in high school then—"

"No, I don't remember." His frown was back. Whatever memories he may or may not have of Gwendolyn Hobbs didn't matter much at the moment. Getting a handle on this *situation* did. Now. "Let me make this clear. My staff is my business. If Marta is taking some time off, then I'll be the one to find a replacement." Because, dammit, he was going to have some say this time.

The dimple disappeared. "Well...I guess..." She cleared her throat. "I understand. Of course." Her gaze darted to the sleeping girls. "I'll figure something else out then." It was almost a whisper. "We'll be fine."

He didn't believe her. Because she didn't. The hint of desperation in her voice had him feeling like an ass. Hell, even Jax looked disappointed in him. The dog's ears perked up. Head cocked sideways. Judging. He could tell.

"It's late." He sighed, exhaustion setting in. "I'm bone-tired. And hungry—"

"Yes. Food." She spun. "Mom told me you would be." The oven opened, the scent of cinnamon and sugar and sweetness flooding the room, and she pulled a small pan out and shot him a timid smile. "It's berry cobbler. Hope you like it?" She slid the pan onto the counter then hurried to the cabinet, on tiptoe for his favorite mug—his favorite mug that she filled to the brim with steaming coffee. She set the mug and a fork beside the small pan and stood back, staring at him with eyes chocolate brown and sparkling with...tears?

Dammit.

LAMBERT DRAEGER WAS going to make her cry. The tell-tale sting in her eyes was embarrassing. But undeniable. No crying. Crying would only make this worse. All she had to do was look at him to know that. Sucking in a deep breath helped. A little.

Fine. Okay. Things weren't turning out the way she'd expected, *but*...they were here. With her mom. Safe and sound. Safe. And...well, that was something.

Now if Lam Draeger would stop scowling at her like some big, manly, angry, gorgeous thundercloud, she might be able to get the girls to their room with some dignity. Maybe. Possibly. If she was smart, she'd avoid looking at him at all. For a variety of reasons.

One, she needed him to like her so she and the girls could stay.

Second, she needed not to stare at him. Because he was worth staring at.

Third...no, that pretty much covered it.

Last time she'd seen him, he wasn't nearly this *impressive*. He'd been a teenager, a cute teenager. That's probably why she hadn't recognized him. When she'd been a painfully awkward adolescent, Lam Draeger had been this older, nice guy, who hadn't picked on her—because he hadn't known she'd existed—whose smile had been like the sun...and...yes, she'd been one of those girls. One of the countless girls in Last Stand who'd been more than a little charmed by the eldest Draeger boy. Especially his smile.

But this Lam was no longer a kid. He was all...man. And he wasn't smiling—like the sun or otherwise. He was glaring. At her. His jaw clenched.

"Not a fan of berry cobbler?" Her voice was thin and high, as if she was recovering from a dental visit that included helium.

"I am." Not that he was happy about it. Not in the least.

"Oh." She knew he was—her mother had told her as much. "I thought you were hungry?"

"I am." He grabbed the fork, scooped up a massive bite, and shoveled it into his mouth. And, suddenly, his scowl disappeared. Melted. His heavy-lidded eyes fluttered close, and his nostrils flared as he sat, heavily, on the wooden stool. He chewed, swallowed, and, sort of, deflated.

"Oh! The ice cream. I made it this evening." She had the wooden bowl with homemade ice cream out of the freezer and on the counter before he could argue. "The girls helped me." With a little force, she formed a perfect scoop and deposited it on his cobbler.

He eyed the ice cream, then glanced her way. "I'm not sure it gets much better than this." He shook his head as his fork tapped the flaky cobbler topping. And there it was. The beginnings of one of those knee-weakening smiles she'd fallen victim to more than once—even though not a single one of those had ever been directed her way.

"Try me," she answered. Her ice cream was perfection, her go-to to impress. And, for no other reason than self-preservation, she needed to impress him. She had no place to go. No job. No money. No options.

If Lam booted her out, well…things couldn't get much worse.

"Go on." The helium voice was back, so she cleared her throat and forced a smile.

One heavy brow arched before he scooped ice cream and cobbler up and into his mouth…and moaned, gruff and thick, and full of appreciation. Good. Maybe she could win him over with cobbler?

She didn't stare at him. Rather, she tried not to. Staring was rude, and the last thing she wanted was to come across as rude. Her mother was the one who came up with the plan and, she'd thought, it was a good plan. Because, honestly, where else was she going to go? But it wasn't much of a plan if Lam didn't approve it. So, staring was out of the question. Because it didn't matter that he'd gone from being a handsome teen to an impossibly gorgeous mountain of a man. All that mattered was the impact he had on her immediate future.

His blue eyes locked with hers. "You're a cook?"

"Chef." She nodded.

"Apple doesn't fall far from the tree." He took another bite.

Considering her mother's culinary talents, that was high praise. "I didn't stand a chance. Growing up, this was the one place where the world made sense. The kitchen, I mean." He was devouring the dessert with gusto, so she kept talking. "No matter what changes were happening in the rest of the world, a great recipe stayed a great recipe. To this day, my great-grandmother's pecan pie is the best I've ever tasted." She nodded at the ice cream. "And ice cream is my specialty. I'm pretty proud of it." Because she'd spent hours perfecting its texture and density.

"You should be." He kept eating.

"Thank you." There was no greater compliment than a clean plate—her mother had taught her that. She enjoyed good food, preparing it and eating it. Which was something her ex had commented on more than once. Their already strained relationship only worsened when he realized she would never be the size six he wanted her to be. Or size eight, for that matter. And she wasn't about to apologize for that, either.

While Lam scraped every bit of berries and cream from the eight-by-eight glass pan, she busied herself with cleanup. Her mother would be up in five hours, and the last thing she needed was a messy workspace.

"I'm guessing Marta's happy to have you home?"

Her mother's smile had been a balm to her wounded soul. There'd been tears, to be sure, but hugs and kisses and sweet smiles, too, because, this time, there was no one and nothing stopping her from coming home.

"Been a while."

"Too long." She nodded, swallowing the thick lump in her throat. How many mothers would welcome in their daughter, and grandchildren, in the middle of the night—no questions asked—after years of next to no communication? Hers had. Her mother had taken them in, fed the girls soup and toast, and listened as Gwen told her an as abridged a version as possible of the situation they'd left behind. But Gwen was up-front about being broke. Completely broke. Her mother had taken another long, awed look at her girls and laid out the plan—her mother would take time off, something she'd never done, to spoil and dote on her granddaughters—and Gwen would step in as the family cook. Her mother's no-nonsense delivery made it all sound so easy. And right.

But, then, she hadn't considered that Lambert Draeger, or any one of the Draegers really, would resist.

"Wouldn't they be more comfortable in a bed?" he asked.

"They're fine." And they were. It was peaceful and quiet and clean here. The pillows were soft and the blankets warm. Her gaze bounced from her sleeping curly-haired daughters to the man sitting across the counter.

He had no right to look at her with such disapproval.

"It's a new place, and they don't like being away from me." She shrugged, wondering why she was explaining herself.

"I don't know how they can sleep," he mumbled.

"The music?" Maybe it was a little loud. But loud music had helped drown out the less-than-suitable sounds from their sketchy neighbors at their former home. Cursing. Screaming. The occasional fight. Yeah, a little swing music had gone a long way to hide the seedier side of their reality. And big band music put a spring in her step. "It's happy."

Which was also true.

But his skepticism—and elevated eyebrows—was hard to miss. "And loud."

He was right. And the reason she usually played it that way no longer existed. Blaring big band music at this time of night probably seemed off to him. Maybe even a little rude, something she needed to avoid being, since it was his house and all. His. Not hers. She needed to remember that. She blew a curl from her forehead and turned the volume down. "Sorry." There was that high, pinched voice again. "Done with that?"

He eyed the empty pan. "Guess so."

She plunged it into the hot, sudsy water and washed it. "I'm glad you enjoyed it." A quick survey told her the kitchen was clean. "Guess I'll turn in."

"Where are you staying?" he asked.

"With Mom." Was that allowed? She worried her lower lip with her teeth, watching him closely. The last thing she wanted to do was to get her mother in trouble.

"How long are you staying?" There was no edge to the question—none she could detect anyway. And he wasn't scowling. Or glaring. He was…curious.

"I'm not sure," she hedged. "I guess that's up to you."

Chapter Two

LAM CIRCLED THE corral, his boots crunching the gravel path. "Fence looks good." He ran his hand along the thick pipe, the newly welded seam barely noticeable. "Where'd you find that kid?"

"Tech school." His brother Kolton nodded. "Jesse's got talent. And he's trying to save money for college."

"Let's throw him more work." If Lam could help this kid get ahead, he would. He and his siblings had grown up lucky. His father might have been a hard man with unreasonably high expectations, but his children never wanted for a thing. "Cattle guard in the north field could be replaced. And we might as well get the chutes in the old barn working again."

"Will do." Kolton started texting. "Damn kids. They won't answer the phone, but they'll fire back a text in no time."

Lam laughed. He'd had the same problem more than once with his brother. Hell, with all of his five siblings.

"Yeah, those *kids*. Hold on, now, where's your cane?" His brother Macon made a big show out of looking around them. "Leave it by your rocker? You keep talkin' like that, you need to start wearing orthotic shoes and a hearing aid."

"Smart-ass." But Kolton was laughing.

They ambled down to the south holding pens. Three large bulls stood, looking downright harmless. "Mad Mike and Jumper are Brahman crossbreeds?" he confirmed. Brahman crossbreeds were a go-to when it came to bucking bulls.

"They are. Tailspin is pure Brahma." Kolton glanced his way. "I know he's not a sure thing but—"

"I said I was up for taking some risks." And he'd meant it. His father's refusal to move their breeding program forward never made any sense to Lam. Now that he was gone…well, things were different.

Kolton's job was to scout out new breeding stock. It wasn't just a matter of a good-looking bull, musculature, or size. Genetics mattered. And Kolton had a good eye—Lam had taught him well. "I'd hoped you'd see it that way."

Lam took the iPad from Macon and scrolled through the spreadsheet with each animal's stats and figures.

"Now all we need are the cows." Macon rested his booted foot on the lowest pipe railing.

Lam remembered the note his sister had left on his desk. "Tabby has a few weddings booked. That whole June bride thing—"

"Seems sorta hot to be walking around in lace and stuff," Kolton interrupted.

Lam chuckled. "Hot or not, folks get married. Check in with Tabby." Lam glanced at his brothers. Their sister was quite the entrepreneur. After working as an event planner in Austin, she'd come home with a notebook full of ideas about expanding the ranch's income sources. Weddings, especially when the peach trees were blooming, were big. They'd built a wedding chapel, then a large barn, adding all sorts of *details* and *elements* that ensured it was a *premiere* event space. Lam didn't know much about fancy weddings, but he did know the business had been steady and, surprisingly, lucrative. And, when it came to Draeger's Weddings & Events, Tabby was all business. And it showed.

"Macon, I need you to do a thorough inspection of the barn and the wedding chapel. We don't want to ruin anyone's special day with a loose floorboard or lighting issue."

Macon nodded. "On it."

"Kolt, you're on grounds duty. Tabby wants the orchard cleaned up for pictures and all that, so make it look…good. She'd mentioned some lattice arch or something. You'll have to ask her." He shrugged.

"No prob." Kolton held his hands up. "Whatever it takes to keep Tabby happy."

Lam smiled.

"Was Marta serious? This morning, I mean?" Macon asked. "She's taking a vacation?"

"Sounded like it." Kolton shook his head. "I get that she wants to help her daughter and all, but I'm not gonna choke down bad food three meals a day."

If her pastries and cobbler were any indication of Gwen's ability in the kitchen, they'd all be fat and happy in no time. Marta was a good cook. Comfort food and lots of it. But the sampling he'd had of Gwen's fare the night before left his taste buds humming. Hints of flavors, layered and rich.

"I remember Gwen. Quiet? Really quiet." Macon turned, his eyes narrowed against the summer sun. "She was in Tabby's class, wasn't she?"

That was news to Lam. He'd laid in bed trying to place Gwen Hobbs in his youth. He had a vague recollection of a shy, round thing that hid in one of the kitchen cabinets. He'd only found that out when he'd discovered *her* there instead of a mixing bowl Marta had been looking for. He'd been in grade school, and the discovery had him falling back onto the floor to knock his head on the corner of the kitchen island. Gwen had burst into tears and run away. It wasn't exactly a warm and fuzzy memory.

Other than that, he remembered nothing.

All he knew of Gwen, the woman, was what Marta had told him—directly and inadvertently. The letters and cards she'd sent to her mother had been treasures Marta had shared with them all. And then, all of a sudden, all communication had stopped. Marta blamed some "smooth talking, no-account good-for-nothing with a pretty face" for her daughter's almost complete disappearance years ago. Lam hadn't asked questions, that wasn't his way.

But he had eyes and ears, and last night had revealed one thing. From the desperation on the woman's face to the broken resignation in her soft voice, Gwen Hobbs needed a place to heal. From what? That was none of his business.

"You really going to let her run the kitchen?" Kolton asked.

Was he? He'd been puzzling over that very question since Marta laid out her plan, in detail, this morning. It was only for a few weeks.

"Has Marta ever taken a vacation before?" Macon pushed off the fence.

"No." Lam sighed. In the entirety of his life, he couldn't

remember a time when Marta Hobbs wasn't cooking in the kitchen.

"Guess she's got plenty of time to take." Kolton shrugged. "She's earned a break. How about we let Gwen cook for us? If it's bad, we can hire on someone else. If she's tolerable, we let her cover for Marta."

Which was basically what he'd come up with. So why was he holding back?

Considering Marta had been around since before they were all born, Marta was family. When her husband had decided to move on, she and Gwen had stayed at the ranch. She'd played a significant role in their upbringing. If one of his brothers smarted off, she had no problem setting them straight. Plus, her long-standing presence and maturity automatically earned respect.

But Gwen? She wasn't the least bit…old. She'd practically danced around his kitchen, feminine and graceful…a downright distraction. And he had been mighty distracted. With her fuzzy socks and striped skirt and mussed hair and big brown eyes…Gwen Hobbs was pretty. No denying it. His brothers were bound to notice, too. Having her in the kitchen, daily, could become problematic. But was there another option?

"Seems fair," Macon said. "Marta has the right to want to spend time with her granddaughters."

Fair, maybe. And while he'd go through with the whole test meal for appearances, he already knew the outcome. Gwen Hobbs would be in his kitchen three meals a day— cooking good food and looking like she did—and he'd just have to come to terms with that.

Lam headed toward the stables, eager for a long, quiet ride. Nothing calmed his nerves like being on horseback.

"Am I the only one who's worried about Gwen?" Kolton was on his heels. "Being gone so long. Showing up in the middle of the night? I don't like secrets, and I get the sense Marta's daughter's got a few of them."

His brother had a valid point. He thought of his father's secret, one he still hadn't fully figured out, and it turned his stomach. He didn't need or want more surprises in his life.

"Talk all you want. Ma's gonna side with Marta on this." Macon followed, too. "She'll do whatever it takes to keep Marta happy and, right here, on the ranch. You know that."

"But it's not just her," Kolton continued. "Is the place even safe for her kids? I mean, what sort of liability are they?"

Macon elbowed Kolton, hard, in the stomach. Whatever else there was to say was cut short.

It was a mistake. But it was out there now—making the air thin and the ground beneath him unsteady. Lam didn't want to think about it, to acknowledge it, but it was there, staring him in the face. It was always there. The pain, jagged and searing, every second of every day. Waking up in the dead of night, searching for what couldn't be found. This hole in his heart would never heal. He'd never heal. But this place, hard work, and his family, made him push through— made him breathe and walk and talk when the grief would bring him to his knees.

Now his brothers were staring at him, searching for the right words to say.

"Lam," Macon murmured.

He did his best to smile. "It's fine. I'm fine." The words

were soft, thick. He cleared his throat. "I'm gonna ride out to check the herd. Pretty sure you two have some work to do, too." He didn't wait to see if they listened. They would. They'd all become skilled at ignoring the giant elephant in the room, dancing around the subject whenever possible.

And he was thankful for it. His son was gone. Grant…he wasn't coming back. And it was Lam's fault. There was nothing else to say.

"MOMMA COOK'N?" JILLY asked, pushing her glasses up her nose.

Gwen nodded. "The question is what?"

"S'ghetti," Amy smiled. "Yummy." She stretched the "m" sound out.

"That's *your* favorite food, Pumpkin Pie." Gwen tapped her daughter on the tip of her little nose. "I could make it for your dinner if you like?"

"Mm-hmm." Amy clapped her hands.

"Stick fish, Momma. Peez, peez, peez." Jilly puckered her lips like a fish, and Amy giggled. "Okay, Gramma?"

"Stick fish?" her mother asked. "Oh, fish sticks."

"Yup, yup, Gramma." Jilly made her fish face again.

Gwen explained, "I've learned that just because they're twins, that doesn't mean they like the same foods. Gwen loves spaghetti. Jilly loves fish sticks. Three years old and they already have very discerning tastes."

"Who doesn't?" her mother asked. "Your momma loved stick fish, too Jilly Ann. And mac and cheese."

"No s'ghetti!" Amy piped up. "Mac and cheez."

"As you can see, they're picky eaters." Gwen teased, shaking her head. "I'm not worried about what to feed you two, though. What about them? The Draegers? I don't know what to make—"

"They're not fancy folk, Gwen." Her mother patted her hand. "They're meat and potato men, through and through. Oh, and dinner rolls. Those boys love their bread." She shrugged. "Pretty easy to keep them happy. Tabby, too." She paused. "Mrs. Draeger's not eating much since…well, she picks like a bird. And she's getting as thin as a scarecrow."

Which hurt Gwen's heart. The Draegers were her mother's family. While she hoped that fact would influence the outcome of tonight's dinner, she knew her cooking needed to speak for itself. To make the Draeger men, especially Lam, happy. But her cooking muse groaned at the idea of making something so pedestrian. If she was going to show off her skillset, why not offer something impressive? "My pastry was the best in my class. I could do a beef Wellington? Or a nice braised leg of lamb?" She paused. "Or coq au vin?"

Jilly squealed. "No legs, Momma."

"No way!" Amy agreed.

Her mother was grinning from ear to ear. "Oh, you two girlies are a hoot."

"Hoot?" Amy blinked.

"Hoot hoot," Jilly ran around the kitchen island chanting.

"Careful, Jilly Bean." Not that she could blame them for being a little stir-crazy. She could go for a nice, long walk herself. To clear her mind and stretch her legs. Her girls, too.

They were full of energy—most three-year-olds were—but there was no place to run it off. Still, there was no forgetting this was a working cattle ranch—with big, mean rodeo bulls. Whatever exploring they did, they'd do it together. "How about you give me a few minutes to figure out what we're cooking, and then we'll all go for a walk?"

"'kay, Momma." Jilly stopped, clasping her hands in front of her.

"Color?" Amy asked, grabbing her twin's hand and tugging her toward the table, where their crayons and coloring books waited. "Wanna picture, Gramma?"

"Yes, please." Her mother flipped through the family cookbook. "Don't worry so much, Gwen. Lam's bent out of shape because he doesn't like surprises."

She'd definitely surprised him, all right. His dark blue eyes had been mercurial. One second, he'd been smiling, the next tight-jawed and snapping. "I got that."

Her mother laughed.

She'd always loved that sound. Her mother's laugh was pure and free. Growing up, this kitchen had been full of laughter.

"The kitchen was remodeled." And what a remodel. Gone were the dated pressboard cabinets and marble-like laminate.

"Mr. Draeger did it." Her mother shrugged. "Mrs. Draeger took a few cooking classes, and he redid the whole space for her. Exactly the way she wanted it."

The only memories she had of Joseph Draeger weren't pleasant. He didn't smile much. Or talk much. He'd been a big man with a stern face and an edge to his every word.

When she'd been little and heard his heavy footfalls coming down the hall, Gwen would hide in the kitchen cabinet she'd cleared out especially for that purpose.

"That man loved to spoil his wife," her mother continued.

"Does she still cook?" Gwen asked.

"No. At the holidays, maybe. Cookies or the like. But she hasn't done much of anything since he passed." Her sigh was heavy.

While Joseph Draeger had terrified her, Adelaide Draeger had mesmerized her. Someone as pretty and delicate as she was didn't seem to belong here. Love wasn't always sensible, though. And the love Adelaide Draeger had for her husband and children was clearly deep and binding.

"I guess it would be hard." Gwen glanced at her mother. "To lose the love of your life but have reminders everywhere?"

Her mother's smile wavered, just a flicker, but it was enough.

"Sorry, Mom." She meant it. Even though her father was alive and well, her mother had lost him. He'd left her—them—picking his career over his family. Her ex...Dominic. Well, his desertion had given her a taste of what that was like. But, for her, there had also been relief that he'd left. She doubted her mother had felt that way when her father had gone.

Her mother patted her hand. "No need. That's long over and forgotten."

Which was a lie. But Gwen recognized her mother's unspoken "end of subject" easily enough. Fine. There was work to be done. Mealtime—her time to shine. "What do you think?"

"About?" Her mother was watching the girls, a smile on her face.

It made her so happy. Her mother, her girls…they'd missed so much time already. That was another reason she needed to win over the Draegers tonight. "My suggestions?" She pulled open the massive chrome refrigerator door for ingredients. "I want dinner to be a sure thing."

"Gwen, honey." Her mother's voice was gentle. "You want a sure thing? Lambert Draeger's favorite meal in the whole wide world is chicken fried steak. Thick-cut steak fries or creamy mashed potatoes with gravy. Corn on the cob and garlic brussels sprouts."

"And dinner rolls?" Gwen finished. "Fine. But I'm going to get creative with dessert."

"I wouldn't expect anything less." Her mother nodded. "Let's take that walk now, before it gets too late."

Dinner was at six thirty, period. She had more than enough time to make dinner—and a chocolate-Chantilly-crème layer cake with more homemade ice cream—and could enjoy a nice walk with her girls.

"You two princesses ready?" Her mother held out her hands, lighting up as Jilly and Amy ran to her. This is what her daughters needed. Right here. Someone else to love them unconditionally. Her girls deserved that.

She followed them down the hall, lingering over the dozens of photos framed along the walls. The Draegers had been a part of Last Stand since its inception. Snippets of the family's long history hung here, matted and framed and preserved, proudly. Some were familiar, some not. One picture drew her to stop. It was a family photo of this generation. Mr. and Mrs. Draeger sat while their children stood behind them. Lambert, Kolton, Macon, Royce, Sam, and Tabitha.

"Who dat?" Amy was tugging at her shirt.

She scooped up her daughter. "This is the Draeger family, Pumpkin. This big house belongs to them."

"Oh." Amy leaned forward, looking at the picture. "Horses here?"

Beside the family photo was a picture of Tabitha, midway through a barrel run. She'd always wanted to be a barrel racer, Gwen remembered that. Looked like her dream came true. "Yes, ma'am. All sorts of animals." She carried Amy down the hall, where her mother and Jilly waited. "But we can't get too close to the animals, girls. They might look pretty, but some of them aren't very friendly."

"Bite us, Momma?" Jilly asked, baring her teeth.

"Let's not find out," she answered.

"Okay, Momma." Jilly wiggled, spinning in a circle.

"Your gramma's right. You are a hoot." She set Amy down.

Her mother laughed. "I can show you the goats. They won't bite. One of them is my pet."

Gwen smiled. Country living. "What's its name?"

"Thumbelina." Her mother's smile grew.

Thumbelina was her favorite fairy tale. Mrs. Draeger had given her a beautifully illustrated copy of the story for her birthday and Gwen had read it over and over, until the binding frayed and the pages came apart.

"Thumba-what?" Jilly asked, making a face.

"Thumbelina," her mother repeated. "It's a story about a little girl having all sorts of adventures." She shot Gwen a quizzical look.

Why hadn't she shared her favorite story with her daughters? Because she didn't want her daughters growing up believing they had to be rescued? Or that they could only be happy when they found their true love? Or maybe it was Thumbelina's restless spirit. All of which was ridiculous.

It was a fairy tale, that's all. A classic, at that.

And, if she was going to overanalyze her beloved bedtime fave, it also taught girls not to settle, no matter how pressured they were, and that kindness and helping others was the right choice. When had she become so jaded? Well, she knew the answer to that. And it made her sad. She didn't want to be the sort of mother who undermined the joy of simple things. Starting now. "Maybe Gramma can read it to you?"

"Peez, Gramma?" Jilly asked.

"Of course." Her mother held the door open, taking hold of Jilly's hand once they were on the wide porch that surrounded the entire ranch house.

Gwen stared out over the rolling hills. For miles, that's all she saw. Hills. Trees. Fences. The occasional cow. Out here, the noise pollution of the city wasn't a thing. The wind, birdsong, and the low hum of cicadas was all there was.

And the barking of a dog.

"Look, Momma!" Amy squealed.

Gwen looked—and instantly regretted it. Lam Draeger,

sleepy-eyed and rumpled was one thing. Starched and pressed and atop a horse, cowboy hat cocked just right, was another. He was, without a doubt, the ideal cowboy.

"A doggie!" Amy squealed again.

Right. The dog. Her daughters would find *that* the interesting thing. Not the impossibly gorgeous man riding a massive dappled gray horse their way, his dog trotting along at his side.

"And a horse," Jilly said, tugging at her mother's hand to get closer. "Big big horse."

"He is." Her mother agreed. "Afternoon, Lambert."

"Miss Marta." Lam touched the brim of his hat, his face in shadows. "Miss…Gwen."

She smiled. "Oh, you know, just Gwen."

"Hi, Cowboy-Man," Jilly said, waving. "Pretty horsie."

"A doggie." Amy clapped her hands together.

The dog's tail wagged with gusto, ears swiveling forward.

"This is Earl." He patted the horse. "And that's Jax. Go on, Jax. Say hello," Lam said to the dog.

The dog trotted forward and sat, tongue lolling out, a doggie-grin on his face.

Amy was so excited, she froze, her eyes wide, mouth open, her little hands clasped tightly together.

"You can pet him," he encouraged.

Amy only blinked.

"Pet him, Amy," Jilly whispered, her sister's nervous energy sending her behind her mother to peer around her legs.

Gwen knelt and held her hand out to Jax. "It's nice to meet you, Jax."

Jax's ears drooped and he came forward, leaning heavily

into her hand.

"Aren't you sweet?" She smiled, giving the dog a good kneading rub. "See, girls? He's a nice puppy. Come say hello."

Jilly didn't let go of her gramma's hand, but she moved close enough to pat Jax's back. The dog gave her little hand a lick, eliciting a full-body giggle from her daughter.

But Amy remained a statue, so Gwen went to her. "What's up, my little pumpkin pie?"

"He's prettiful," she whispered, her gaze fixed on Jax. "And real, right, Momma?"

"He's real," Lam answered. She could hear the smile in Lam's voice. "Jax helps me herd the cattle, lets me know if there's any danger, and takes care of me."

"Hurt?" Amy repeated, her lower lip trembling.

"No, no, sweetie." Gwen shook her head. "Herd. Herd. It means help move all the cows from one place to another. Right, Mr. Draeger?"

"Lam." He paused. "Yes, ma'am, that's right. Ol' Jax here wouldn't hurt a fly."

Amy thought that was the funniest thing she'd ever heard. Her laugh rang out so much that Jax couldn't resist. He came right up to her and gave her a kiss on the cheek. Amy reached out one hand, so in awe of the dog, she moved in slow motion. Her little fingers sank into his fur, gently.

"That's nice, Amy." She smiled at her daughter. "See, he likes it. His tail says so."

Both girls peered at Jax's thumping tail.

"Heading out?" Lam asked.

"We thought we'd take a stroll down to the tank and let

the girls run a bit," her mother answered.

Lam let out a heavy sigh. "Take Jax. It's been awfully dry." He nodded. "Stay on the path—no poking around in the rocks."

Gwen was pretty sure that meant something but didn't want to ask in front of the girls.

"Will do." Her mother nodded. "You ready, girlies? Come on, Jax."

Gwen stood, watching the smiles on her mother and daughters' faces. And the laughter? Sweetest sound in the world. Nothing compared to that. Not even the presence of Lam Draeger in all his cowboy-hotness. Not that he didn't cut a fine picture, because he did. But she'd made a promise to herself last night: if she was going to work here, she'd have to ignore Lam's overwhelming good looks. Period. She would be the consummate professional. "Have a nice afternoon." She gave him a little wave and followed her family, feeling more awkward than professional.

"Gwen." He cleared his throat.

She shielded her eyes from the bright Texas sun, peering up at him. "Yes?" She couldn't resist adding, "Cowboy-Man." So much for keeping it professional. His chuckle was soft, but she heard it.

"Might be a good idea to get the girls some boots."

Which, if she remembered correctly, weren't cheap.

"Hats might not be a bad idea, either." He paused. "It would keep the sun out of your eyes, too."

Because buying three-year-olds cowboy hats was the most practical thing in the world. But, he was a Draeger, and chances were they'd have very different ideas of what was an essential purchase. "I'll figure something out. But I appreci-ate the advice."

"Just keep them on the path." He turned. "Jax'll let you know if there are any snakes around."

"Right." She did her best to sound nonchalant, even though her heart had jumped into her throat. "Sure. Snakes." She gave up and ran after her girls, hoping like hell Lam was teasing but not willing to risk it.

Chapter Three

"I CAN'T BELIEVE you're here." Tabby was gushing, something his sister rarely did. Apparently, she and Gwen had been in the same grade. And the same class. And the same scout troop. They'd been hugging on and off for the last ten minutes. Yes, there were years between him and his sister, but he couldn't help feeling like a jerk for not knowing any of this.

Gwen shrugged. "I know. It's weird. In a good way. Things just finally worked out, and here we are."

"And I've never been happier in my life," Marta added, looking at her daughter with sheer adoration.

Gwen stopped whisking long enough to kiss her mother's forehead. "Me, too, Mom."

"Me, too." Gwen's daughter chimed in, smiling as she pushed her glasses up her little nose.

"Me, too, too." The other one added, her smile shy.

"It's unanimous then." Tabby spun the stool to face Gwen's girls. "They look so much like you, Gwen. It's like being back in Mrs. Quintero's room all over. Just adorable."

"Wow, Mrs. Quintero? Kindergarten?" Gwen laughed. "I do miss coloring and recess. Oh, and naptime."

"Naptime should be a thing, no matter how old you are," Marta agreed.

Lam leaned against the doorframe, listening. Between the women's easy banter and occasional laughs and the incredible smell of whatever Gwen was cooking, he was in no hurry to leave. Besides, watching Gwen's girls was pretty entertaining. The one with the glasses was swinging her feet back and forth and humming while she scooped up her mac and cheese. She was Jilly? Or Jilly Bean? That's what Gwen called her.

The other one, the one Jax was especially partial to, was eating her mac and cheese one noodle at a time. The tip of her tongue stuck out as she concentrated on every bite. It was pretty damn cute. Shy Amy. Or Pumpkin Pie—another nickname. Every once in a while, Amy would look up, see him, smile, and go back to eating.

They were cute. Adorable. So adorable that he'd ended up changing his plans and circling around back to the house in the off chance they needed help.

They hadn't, of course. But he had to be there. Which was something he'd have to get over—if they stayed. Who was he kidding? Since they were staying.

"Don't you think, Lam?" Tabby asked.

All eyes were on him, waiting for his answer to a question he hadn't heard. "Tuned out," he admitted.

"Of course, you did." His sister rolled her eyes. "I said Jax seems awful sweet on Miss Amy."

He nodded.

"He is prettiful," Amy said, staring down at the dog laying on the floor at her feet.

"Is he now?" Tabby asked. "Never really thought of him that way. But I guess you're right, Amy. Jax is handsome."

"Han-some?" Jilly stopped eating. "What that?"

"It means pretty. Or beautiful." Gwen stopped whisking again. "For boys, mostly."

Jilly and Amy looked at each other, both of them mulling over this piece of information.

"Can I get you something, Lambert?" Marta asked. "A drink? Gwen has some cookies about ready to come out of the oven, if you can't wait for dinner?"

That was the smell. His stomach growled, loudly, but he shook his head. He had five women staring at him, wearing a range of expressions—all expectant. "She dragged me in here." He nodded at his sister, bristling. He shouldn't need an excuse to be in his kitchen, should he? Just because he didn't make a habit of hanging out in here before, that didn't mean he couldn't now.

"Guilty as charged." Tabby raised her hand. "I was excited. You can go do whatever it is you do, if you like, big brother."

"Or you can stay," Marta said, a smile creasing her face. "Have a seat. Chat awhile."

Gwen glanced up, spooning batter into a pan. Chocolate. Like her eyes.

His stomach growled again, and Gwen's smile grew until that damn dimple appeared. Her brown eyes bounced his way, long enough to make his chest tight. "Right." He surveyed the room, nodded once, pushed the kitchen door wide, and walked out of the kitchen and into the great room, away from Gwen's brown eyes and dimples.

"Scouting out the situation?" Kolton asked, looking up from the cattle breeder's magazine he was reading.

"Not exactly. Tabby." He shrugged. "One minute we were standing there talking, the next she found out Gwen was here, and she was hauling me into the kitchen with her."

"Sounds about right." Kolton frowned. "Wait. Why was she hauling you into the kitchen?"

"They know each other."

"Great. Just great." Kolton turned back to his magazine. "We're gonna end up eating burnt food, having to be on our best behavior, with kids running around, aren't we?"

"Still worrying about your stomach?" Macon came into the room. "You know, you could give the girl a chance."

"She's not a girl," Lam mumbled. Gwen Hobbs was undeniably a woman. A woman with dimples and sweet smiles and warm, chocolate eyes.

Kolton perked up, a crooked grin appearing. "Interesting. You're saying she's pretty?"

Lam cursed under his breath.

Macon's brows rose. "Is she? If she is, maybe you'll be able to choke down her cooking after all."

"I just meant she's a...woman." He needed to stop talking. His brothers were watching him closely. Too closely. If he'd just kept his mouth shut. The only person he had the right to be irritated with was himself. "She's, you know, a mother."

"Uh-huh." Kolton was up, smoothing his shirt front and checking the large wooden clock over the massive stone fireplace.

"Cool it, you've got thirty minutes to go." Macon shot his brother a look.

"What's happening in thirty minutes?" Their mother

chose that moment to join them, dressed for dinner—her smile tired. She had aged a good ten years in the months since their father's death. She'd always said he was her sun and moon and stars, and losing him had definitely taken a toll on her.

"Kolton's planning on charming Marta's daughter." Macon laughed. "Poor Gwen."

Kolton did have that look on his face, the one that caught the attention of every woman in the room. His brother had a way with the opposite sex. And Lam had just made it open season on Gwen. Damn it all.

"Lam thinks she's attractive," Macon added.

His mother stared at him. "You do?"

What the hell? "I never said a word about her looks." He did his best not to sound irritated. Irritation would only fuel his brothers teasing, and he was already too out of sorts to handle their digs well.

"Well?" His mother was doing her best not to smile. "Is she?"

"Is she what?" He knew, of course. But, if he was lucky, she'd drop it.

"Attractive?" Her blue eyes pinned his.

Yes. Attractive wasn't enough. Answering her question felt like knowingly stepping on a bear trap. Hedging was his only option. "I guess." He shook his head. "I've got some phone calls to return. I'll see you all at dinner."

"Lambert." She caught his arm. "Don't go. Please. I thought we were all teasing. I didn't mean to chase you off." Her gaze swept over his face, her expression shifting. "Sometimes, I see so much of your father in you."

Six months ago, he might have considered that a compliment. But now? What would his mother say if she knew her husband had been sending money, monthly, to a woman in Mesquite Creek, Arizona? Whoever she was, his father had gone to great pains to keep her a secret. Lam had hired a private detective to track her down.

Even though learning who and why his father was sending money to this person was an inevitability, he feared it would forever change the way he viewed his dad. And, hard as Joseph Draeger had been, Lam had loved his father dearly. Something about his reserved nature made Lam—made all of his children—work hard to earn some sort of acknowledgement.

Lam's bull riding years had made him the family golden boy. No matter how many bones he'd broken, his father's encouragement had him riding as soon as the doctor cleared him. If he'd managed to roll a few more feet, he would have avoided the hoof of the seventeen-hundred-pound bull that shattered his right femur. He hadn't. And, along with the end of his bull riding career, he'd wound up with a leg full of pins and rods and a gait that grew awkward when rain or cold set it. His father had also taken the loss of Grant hard and made sure Lam knew just how disappointed he was over Lam's divorce shortly thereafter. It hadn't exactly been a cake walk for Lam either.

Kolton had rodeo in his veins, too. He'd been one hell of an all-around cowboy, earning prize money and belt buckles all over the state. He still team roped now and then, but seeing Lam's constant injuries and slow recovery had dampened his enthusiasm for competing—disappointing their

SWEET ON THE COWBOY

father.

But the two of them had stepped up at home, shouldering the majority of the ranch management and lessening the divide between them and their father.

Not that they were the only ones hoping to gain their father's favor.

Macon split his time between the ranch, doing fix-it jobs around town when the need arose, and Last Stand's fire department. It was that last bit that their father had loved bragging about most.

Royce? He was a Marine—deployed God knows where for the last four years. Their father couldn't have been prouder.

Tabitha didn't stand a chance. Their father was old-fashioned, and she was his only daughter. It didn't matter that she'd graduated with honors, participated in several international Leaders of Tomorrow summits, or earned her master's degree in record time, their father wanted her to marry and have grandchildren. Period. As a result, Tabby hadn't had a serious boyfriend... ever.

And Sam. Well, they didn't talk about Sam. To their father, Sam ceased to exist about five years ago. And he'd forbidden anyone, ever, to talk about him. They'd all tried to reach out to their brother, hiding it from the father, of course. He was in jail, not dead, but Sam had sent back their letters and refused their visits until they'd given up. Sam's involuntary manslaughter conviction and seven-year prison sentence had devastated his parents, but Sam hadn't denied the fight—or the resulting death. Lam still wrote the occasional letter, hoping. So far, they'd all come back. It was something he'd blamed his father for—for being so hard-hearted toward his own son. Lam couldn't imagine it.

They hadn't always agreed with what their father said or how he'd done things, but they'd all tried so hard to earn their father's respect. Lam was only now beginning to wonder if the man deserved it.

"Lam?" His mother's palm pressed to his cheek. "Where did you go?" She smiled.

"Nowhere." He smiled back, taking her hand in his. "Just thinking. I really do have some phone calls to make."

She shook her head. "You work too hard, Lambert. It's not good for you, you know?"

Maybe not, but it kept him going. He was still adjusting to being the one in charge of Draeger Ranch, but one thing was certain: he wasn't about to let it fall apart under his watch. Now he could do what he'd wanted to do—breed rodeo stock, bulls and broncs, as well as beef cattle. It would be a challenge, but one that he wanted to take on. Besides, the place—and the people—gave him purpose. "I get plenty of fresh air and exercise." He winked.

"Tabby told me about the big, fancy wedding coming up. In three weeks." His mother said, "You boys make sure the orchard is looking its finest. To hear Tabby talk, this one wedding will bring in more than all the others she's booked combined."

"Already on it," Macon nodded. "You know Tabby, cracking that whip."

"Anyone we know?" Lam asked.

"That's a question for your sister." She smiled. "So, be-sides being pretty, what do you think of Marta's daughter?"

He glanced at the clock. "You can make your own opinions in about fifteen minutes. I'm going to make those phone calls now."

Part of him had been dreading tonight's meal all day. Gwen Hobbs made him nervous, and he wasn't sure what to do or how to handle it. But the other part of him, the part he needed to ignore, was looking forward to dinner. And it had nothing to do with the food.

GWEN STRAIGHTENED THE fork, running her fingers along the carefully folded napkin.

"You really pulled out all the stops, Gwen," Tabby said, assessing the table. "You know this is a sure thing, don't you? I mean, of course, it is. You're a chef. And family."

Her mother might be, but she was not. And Lam had made it clear this wasn't a sure thing. Not that she was going to point that out to Tabby. She was his sister. "I guess we'll see."

"And you look so nice."

Gwen stared down, in horror. "I didn't change."

"You were going to change?" Tabby shook her head. "This is a family dinner not a five-star restaurant. Okay? You *do* look nice."

She loved her bright yellow dress covered with tiny red strawberries. It was soft and utterly feminine—she'd bought it for that reason. As far as she was concerned, the fashion of the nineteen forties was one of the most feminine of all times—even for curvy women. Classic elegance, Hollywood glamour, with touches of whimsy and tailored details. From pencil skirts to belted dresses, rhinestone pins to seamed hose, fancy hairstyles and dramatic lipstick, she loved it all. It was Gwen's way of making every day more fun—more *her*. But, according to Dominic, her fondness for retro fashion emphasized the width of her hips. His words had left an impression, one that made her wish she'd had time to change into something different.

"Too late now," she murmured. She'd just keep her apron on… But it was covered with smears of chocolate, batter from the chicken fried steak, and butter.

Tabby must have seen the panic on her face because she smiled. "Gwen, I mean it. You look pretty—like you walked off the cover of a nineteen forties magazine ad. You're going to have to show me how you do all that." She pointed at Gwen's intricate hairdo. "Stop worrying. The food smells incredible. The dessert looks like a mouth orgasm. There's even flowers on the table." She took her hands and squeezed. "Breathe."

Gwen did. A long deep breath. Followed by another. "Did you say mouth orgasm? I've never heard that one. Foodgasm, yes."

"Same thing." Tabby shrugged. "One suggestion?"

She nodded.

"Lose the apron." She pointed at the streaks of chocolate. "Pretty sure that's when the girls helped lick out the bowl."

"Pretty sure you're right." Gwen untied the strings and slipped the loop over her neck, feeling more self-conscious than she had in years. Damn Dominic and his opinions anyway.

The kitchen door opened and she didn't have time to think about Dominic anymore. The Draegers were all dizzyingly gorgeous people. She shoved the apron in the cabinet she used to hide in, smoothed her hands over the front of her dress, and tried to smile.

"Gwen?" Mrs. Draeger shook her head, crossing to her without a second's hesitation. "Look at you. All grown up and just lovely."

Gwen was enveloped in a perfume-scented hug. A crushing, lingering hug, scented with ashes of roses. Gwen hugged back. Adelaide Draeger was skin and bones. Too skinny.

"Welcome home, darling." The woman held Gwen at arm's length, her blue eyes sweeping from head to toe. "Just lovely."

Gwen brushed aside the compliment. "Let's hope you feel the same way about dinner."

"I'm sure I will." Mrs. Draeger looked at the table. "Flowers? You picked flowers?"

Gwen paused. She and the girls, never leaving the path, had collected a vivid armful of wildflowers she'd tried to turn into a pleasing arrangement. "Flowers finish a meal," she said, fully aware that Lam and his dashing brothers were openly staring at her.

"Macon?" She smiled. Macon still looked like the Macon she remembered. Bigger. Brawnier. But his smile was still easygoing. He'd always had a good soul and a gentle heart.

"Gwen." He grinned. "Good to see you."

"You, too." She held her hand out.

He took it, shaking it. "This is weird."

She laughed. "It's called being professional."

"We're all family here." Kolton held his arms wide.

There was no way she was hugging Kolton Draeger. He might not remember blaming her for breaking one of his mother's teacups, but she did. It had been mortifying. Absolutely horrible. She'd stood, shaking, in front of Mr. Draeger, while he held out the remaining pieces of the cup and asked her if she knew what happened to it. She wasn't about to rat Kolton out for playing ball in the house. He, however, had no qualms saying she'd tripped and fallen into the cabinet—breaking the cup.

"I didn't have time to change." She shrugged, hoping he'd take the hint.

He didn't. It wasn't a big deal, really. Kolton had always considered himself far more charming than he actually was. And there were quite a few girls who'd shared his opinion of himself. Too bad she wasn't one of them. Still, she patted his back, and did her best to arch away from him.

Over his shoulder, she saw Lam. He was scowling, his eyes narrowed, jaw locked tight—downright fuming.

"Dinner's ready," she said, stepping away from Kolton. "You all find your seats."

She spent the next few minutes serving up perfectly crisp chicken fried steak, smooth-as-silk mashed potatoes, and all the trimmings. It was good. She knew it was. She'd tried it. But she waited, lingering beside Tabby's chair.

"Pull up a seat," Kolton encouraged.

Which wasn't expected.

"Your mother joins us whenever she wants to," Mrs. Draeger offered. "We'd be happy to have you eat with us, Gwen. The girls too. I'm sure I'm not the only one who'd like to catch up."

Was it her imagination, or did Adelaide Draeger just shoot Lam a rather meaningful look? And, what, exactly, did that look mean?

"You didn't eat with the girls," Tabby offered. "Sit."

She was about to argue when Lam stood, crossed the kitchen, rifled through the cabinets, and headed to the stove. Minutes later he set a full plate, knife and fork, and napkin on the table between him and Tabby. He didn't look her way or say a word. He just...took care of it. He sat down, put his napkin in his lap, and waited.

"Thank you," she murmured, feeling acutely uncomfortable as she slid into her chair. She had enough food for two adult men on her plate, but she wasn't going to read anything into that. Even if it immediately killed her appetite. "Please, go on. I tend to taste as I go, to make sure it's good." She shrugged and smiled. "It's good."

Kolton cut into his steak and took a big bite. "Damn good."

"Kolton." His mother's tone was disapproving. "Language. *And* your mouth is full."

"Sorry, Mom. It's that good." He pointed at her plate with his fork. "Eat up."

Would she eat? This might be her son's favorite meal, but something told Gwen that Adelaide Draeger had different tastes.

"Don't get your feelings hurt if she doesn't eat," Tabby whispered.

"She doesn't eat," Lam added, casting a glance his mother's way.

"You're worried about her?" And it touched her heart.

His blue eyes met hers. Wary almost. Definitely searching. As if he was determined to pick her apart? To find a reason to send her away? His gaze wandered, exploring her face with care, before their gazes locked once more, and the crease between his brows slowly smoothed. His lips parted and he shifted closer, like he had something to say. Leaning toward him was instinctual.

"You're looking serious, Lam," Kolton interrupted. "Leave the poor girl alone and eat. Eat. That'll make up your mind for you."

Lam's gaze fell from hers to his plate, as if he was seeing the food for the first time. "You're not playing fair." Those blue eyes were back. Only this time, the corners were creased—from a blinding smile.

She wasn't playing fair? Oh, come on. This...he...wasn't fair. Not in the least.

Here she sat, rumpled with who knows what cooking stains on her dress—she hadn't even been able to touch up her lipstick—and he was smiling. Like that.

And, finally, taking a bite of her cooking.

The food was good. Very good. She'd made sure of it. But she still found herself holding her breath until he closed his eyes and moaned.

"Mm." He shook his head.

"Exactly." Macon laughed.

"What did you mean, Kolton? About Lam making up his mind?"

Mrs. Draeger's question earned her full attention. Didn't she know this meal was a job interview? Surely Lam would have run that by her—since this was her kitchen. The kitchen Mr. Draeger had renovated for her to use when, or if, she wanted.

"I'm fairly certain her cooking abilities have nothing to do with how your brother feels about Gwen's looks." Mrs. Draeger was smiling. "It's not like he'd suddenly find her unattractive if she'd burned dinner. Oh, you can't imagine how many times your father sat through an inedible meal just to please me."

Wait a minute.

It took every ounce of her self-control not to look at the man sitting immediately to her right. Which was a lot. Because he was right there and gorgeous and, apparently, thought she was attractive?

He thought that? And told his mom?

No. Lam Draeger didn't strike her as the sort of man who would share that sort of information with his mother. Which meant, clearly, Mrs. Draeger had seriously misunderstood something. She shook her head, spearing one of the garlic butter brussels sprouts with the tines of her fork. "I'm glad you like it."

"So, Gwen, what have you been up to?" Kolton asked. "Your mom told us about cooking school, but that's been a couple of years."

She forced her smile to stay in place. If this was a normal job interview, these were the sort of questions she'd never be asked. But, for now, this was her only option, so she'd have to make the best of it. "I met a guy working at a restaurant. I had two kids. The job didn't work out. The guy didn't work out. The kids did, thank goodness, since I can't imagine life without them."

And just like that, the room went absolutely silent. Loaded and awkward, stretching on until she was scared to breathe. Worse, she didn't know what she'd said or who she'd upset. Everyone at the table was suddenly engrossed with their plates, carefully avoiding eye contact.

"The meal was very good." Lam broke the silence.

"It was incredible," Macon added. "I admit, I've been eyeing that cake since we sat down."

"She made ice cream, too," Tabby said.

Apparently, the spell was broken. Whatever she'd said or done, Lam had swept it aside. But it had happened—and she had no idea what *it* was. And if she didn't find out what it was, she could never prevent it from happening again.

"You know the drill," Kolton said, standing. "I'm thinking Marta told you?"

She waited, staring around at the Draegers for some clue.

"You cook, we clean." Kolton smiled.

"He means rinse and load our plates into the dishwasher," Tabby murmured. "I'm pretty sure Kolton has never actually washed a dish in his life."

"Well, it's something." Gwen stood, carrying her dishes to the counter. She ended up shooing Kolton and Macon aside. In her experience, the less people in the way, the better. It was her place—her comfort zone—she didn't like it being invaded. She turned to load a plate and backed into Lam, then turned to face him. "Oops."

"You didn't eat." He looked at her plate.

"I'm fine. I've got reserves." She hated the words. Hated how easily she said them and how instantly they diminished her.

He frowned.

"I'll serve dessert." Her words ran together. "Would you take the dessert plates to the table?"

He was still frowning, but he did as she asked.

When the cake was cut and the ice cream was served and the noises of overall approval filled the kitchen, Gwen started to relax.

"What are we celebrating?" Macon asked.

She looked back and forth between them, confused.

"This is a special-occasion dessert," Kolton explained.

She laughed, tucking one of the curls that had slipped free from her bun behind her ear. "So, you're saying I can take it down a notch from now on?"

"Nope." Kolton shook his head.

"You better. My jeans won't thank you." Tabby grinned.

"It was a delicious meal, Gwen. From beginning to end," Mrs. Draeger agreed. "The cake is pure decadence." Considering there were only crumbs left on her plate, Gwen was pleased. Adelaide Draeger had a sweet tooth—Gwen could help with that.

"You'll have to tell me some of your favorite recipes." She was up and clearing plates, already making up lists of treats in her head to tempt Adelaide into eating. Better to be safe than sorry. "Oh, also, any food allergies? Things you really don't like. That's just as important when planning menus."

Kolton and Adelaide thanked her again before escaping any further clean-up duty. She didn't mind. She had plans to make. Now that she knew chocolate was a win, breakfast tomorrow was either chocolate croissants or chocolate chip pancakes. She washed and dried the pots and pans she'd used, making note of her ingredients, and how soon she and the girls would need to do some shopping.

She didn't know why she was so hesitant about leaving the ranch. Dominic was in New York. He would never, ever, come to Texas—not even to find his daughters. Would he?

"Gwen?" Macon touched her shoulder. "Did you hear me?"

"What?" She jumped. "Sorry."

"You and Lam," he muttered, shaking his head.

"What about us?" she asked, Adelaide Draeger's earlier comment still rattling around in her head.

"You both get lost in your own thoughts." He shrugged, studying her.

She glanced at Lam, wiping down the table. "I'm guessing we're thinking about very different things."

"Try me," Lam said, standing.

"What to make for breakfast." She paused, eyebrow arched.

"Chocolate croissants or chocolate chip pancakes." He nodded. "Mom *is* partial to chocolate."

She stared, in absolute shock. How could he possibly know what she'd been thinking? "How?" she asked.

Macon burst into laughter and hurried from the room.

"Tabby?" she pleaded.

"I can't, Gwen. Look how much he's enjoying this." Tabby hugged her, grinning mischievously. "Dinner was amazing. See you in the morning?"

She faced Lam. "Well?"

One of those smiles. Yup, there goes the sun. "Well, what?"

Oh, he was so enjoying himself. And, honestly, if he kept smiling like that, she'd be pretty happy herself. That smile had her grinning right back at him.

"You were talking. Out loud." He cleared his throat. "You and Marta work out her time off, and we'll get you set up on the payroll."

"Really?" she whispered.

He nodded.

How she crossed the room so fast was a mystery. And twining her arms tight around his waist for a no-holding-back hug was an equal puzzle. One minute she'd been holding a wet sponge, the next she was clinging to Lam Draeger as if her life depended on it.

They could stay. She could breathe.

But then she was wrapped in the warmth of his arms, pulled close against the wall of his chest, and the hows and whys no longer mattered.

"Hey," his voice was low and gruff, his breath brushing against her temple. "Are you okay, Gwen?"

She pressed her eyes closed, burying her face against his chest. Was she? Other than the launching herself at her *boss* thing? She breathed deep. She *would* be okay now that she had a place to regroup. Thanks to him.

But it *wasn't* fair that, now that she had launched herself at him, she liked having his arms around her.

"I'm fine." With herculean strength, and instant regret, she pulled free of his hold. "Thank you for this opportunity, Lam." She swallowed. Holding his gaze was a real struggle when he wasn't scowling at her. The way he was looking at her now was an entirely different sort of look. Warm. Curious. Maybe even concerned. For her?

"And I'm sorry. For that," she whispered. He needed to stop looking so genuinely concerned about her. She was trying to be professional. Crying wasn't professional. "Guess my emotions got the best of me. It's a relief. A huge relief. That was...well, I'm sorry. It won't happen again?" Why did that sound like a question? She wasn't asking him. She was telling him—and herself—that this was a mistake.

Now she had to convince herself that was true.

The muscle in his jaw twitched, but he nodded. "Right. Well. Good night." But he lingered, still studying her.

"What did I decide?" she asked. "About breakfast tomorrow."

"Pancakes." A crooked smile had her insides melting. "Mom will like that."

"Chocolate chip pancakes it is." She bit into her lower lip, but it didn't stop her answering smile.

He nodded again—his jaw muscle so tight, she worried he'd cause himself permanent damage—and walked out of the kitchen.

Chapter Four

THE GLOW OF his beside clock said two twelve. Outside, the moon was high. Inside, the house slept. Well, everyone but him. He'd been tossing and turning for the last two hours but was too stubborn to do anything about it.

But, dammit, tonight had knocked everything sideways. Because of her. Gwen. He'd even skipped his late-night snack, to Jax's disappointment, and tried to get some work done. Not that he'd been all that successful. About midnight, he'd dodged the kitchen and headed to bed.

Sleep wasn't coming, his stomach was growling, and his mind wouldn't shut off. He was going to have to break his late-night snacking habit eventually. But tonight wasn't that night. Besides, by now the coast should be clear. He threw back the quilt and sat up, ran a hand through his hair, and yawned.

On his mat, Jax snored softly. His kitchen raid looked to be a solo endeavor…until he pulled on his pants and opened his bedroom door. Then Jax popped up and trotted after him.

"Guess you're hungry, too?" he whispered.

Jax's tail wagged.

"Figured."

They navigated the dark with ease. His father had been a

creature of habit—things tended to stay the same around here. That included every piece of furniture they owned. Maybe it was time to redecorate?

Tabby would be up for that. She was all into fashion and decorating and that stuff. He wondered if his mother was ready for a change. Chances are, she'd fight him simply because everything in the house was tied to his father. He couldn't exactly explain to her that was the reason he wanted to get rid of most of it. Or to his siblings.

He was still mulling over ways to present the idea to his mother when he pushed into the kitchen.

The light over the stove was the only light on, but it was more than enough. Gwen was wearing near-neon rainbow pajamas, leaning forward on the counter, several cookbooks open and spread out before her. She was tapping her foot, humming something—off tune—with enthusiasm. Her long, curly hair swayed in time with her foot tapping.

"Perfect," she said, patting one book and clapping her hands in delight.

He grinned, her childlike excitement making him wonder what had her so fired up. Apparently, Jax was thinking the same thing because he trotted across the floor, sat, and pawed at Gwen's calf with a soft whimper.

She screamed—almost. She caught herself, covering her mouth before she woke the house. "Jax, you scared me to death. What are you doing here, sneaking around?" She stooped, rubbing Jax behind the ear. "Are you hungry? Did Cowboy-Man not feed you? Poor baby. I bet I can find you something yummy."

Her instant assumptions forced him to say, "*We* were

hungry."

She jumped again and, in her crouched position, she slipped and landed hard on her rear, on the floor. "Lam. You scared me." She pressed a hand to her chest. "Both of you."

He was already crossing the floor, holding out his hand to her. He helped her up, liking the feel of her soft, silky hand in his. And he liked the way she smiled up at him, her curls a mess, that dimple peeking out—almost happy to see him. He liked all of it a little too much.

"Thank you," she said, tugging her hand away and smoothing her voluminous pajama top.

He nodded, managing to mumble, "Hungry." What was he? A caveman? So, she got to him. She was pretty. And it had been a long time since he'd really noticed a woman. But it wasn't the first time he'd found a pretty woman in his kitchen in the middle of the night. Okay, that was a lie. He'd never been in this predicament before. Not that her oversized pajamas were remotely enticing. They weren't. *She* was. Still, he could speak in complete sentences. "We missed our snack."

She blinked, fidgeting on her bare feet, pulling her hair over her shoulder. Her gaze fell from his face to his bare chest. "You're hungry?"

He nodded. Was he? He was. That was why he'd come in here. Now? He wasn't hungry. Now he was all twisted up inside. Which wasn't like him, not at all. The realization was a gut-punch. Because he was a fool. He should go. Now.

He didn't.

"I wasn't expecting anyone this late," she murmured, practically running across the room. "But I'm glad you're here. I've been working on something." With a flip of the switch, the lights over the kitchen sink came on. Big mistake. Her pajamas, even in the dark, were bright. With the lights on, they were blinding.

"I left my sunglasses in my room." He held up his arm, pretending to shield his eyes.

"Ha ha, very funny." She rolled her eyes.

He thought so, he was smiling, relaxing—a little. "What did you make me?"

"Not for you, really." She smiled, glancing over her shoulder as she opened the oven. "I've been thinking about your mom since dinner. About how worried you are. She is too skinny, which is something I know nothing about." Her laugh was forced. "I thought, maybe, I could work on fattening her up a bit? Not like me—I mean...in a healthy way, of course. I'll start with desserts, since she seems partial to them."

As usual, she'd put a whole lot of information out there real fast. But a few things jumped out at him. She was up late concocting a plan to get some weight on his mother? And, wait, she thought she was fat? Was she serious? To him, she was everything a woman should be.

Her brown eyes met his, waiting for some sort of acknowledgement. "If that's okay? Maybe?"

Getting his mother to eat? That was more than okay. But the rest of what she'd said? "Maybe." He wasn't sure what had him more rattled, her thoughtfulness about his mother, or her self-demeaning comments. He stood there, awkwardly, searching for some way to address the rest of what she'd said but coming up empty.

"You think so?" she asked. And she smiled, dimples and white teeth. Warning bells were ringing. "I'm glad. Try these petit fours and see what you think." She carried the plate to the table. "Or, there are some oatmeal raisin cookies, if you'd rather. I got carried away with the baking."

She was still smiling. Which he liked. "No."

"No? You don't want to try them?" She frowned. "Or, no, you don't want the oatmeal raisin cookies?"

"How about I try these petite thingies, and I get a cookie?" He smiled.

She chuckled and set the plate down. "I think that can be arranged. Milk?"

Instead of admiring the curve of her cheek and the long sweep of her dark lashes, he focused on the buttons of her pajamas. Clouds. "Where did you get those?"

"Don't hate on the pajamas." She crossed her arms. "My girls have excellent taste."

He nodded. "Talk about a mother's love."

"They have matching pajamas," she explained, pulling the milk from the fridge and pouring him a glass. "How could I say no? They outnumber me, after all. And when they want something, it's pretty hard to resist." She put the milk back. "They never ask for anything, either, so...yeah." She held out the shirt and shrugged.

"Thank you." He took the milk. "I probably would've said yes, too."

"Now that would have been a sight." She shook her head, laughing. "I guess I'm talking too much."

He didn't mind.

"Aren't you going to try them?" She pointed at the little

cakes on the plate.

"They look too pretty to eat." He stared at them. "You did this?"

"It's what I do." She sat in the chair beside him. "Looks are important, but the taste is the key." She rested her elbows on the table. "So?"

"So?" he asked back.

"Take a bite." She pushed the plate closer, eyes wide. "I think she'll like this one best. White chocolate. See the little detail there? Like a tiny berry?" She picked it up and held it out for inspection, smiling.

He stared at the cake she was holding out. "That's something."

She laughed. "I'm not even sure what that means."

"It means it makes my eyes cross looking at it, much less trying to imagine putting frosting and..." He swirled his finger at the cake. "And all that on something so little. Now I'm supposed to eat it?"

"It's cake. Being eaten is the reason for its existence." Her brows rose high. "Go on, try it." He heard the hint of uncertainty in her voice.

For all her eye rolling and big smiles, she wasn't as confident as she came across. And if there was something he understood, it was putting on a brave face for others. It was hard work, exhausting.

With a nod, he held his hand out. "If you insist."

She nodded, placing the cake in his open palm, the tips of her fingers grazing his skin and making her cheeks turn a soft pink.

WHAT IF HE didn't like it? She'd tasted it, she knew each one of them was delicious. But, still, Lam's opinion mattered.

She'd watched Mrs. Draeger tonight and, now, like Lam, she was worried over the woman's fragile state. Maybe feeding her cakes and chocolate pancakes was a stopgap, but it was a start.

"Is it because of your dad?" she asked. "The whole not eating thing?"

The cake paused, inches from his lips. He nodded. "His death hit her hard. But I guess, after forty-some years, that's to be expected."

She nibbled on her lower lip.

She and Dominic hadn't spent five years together, and it had been more than enough. Forty years? That was two lifetimes. How would it be to lose someone you'd shared so much with? Built a life with? A home and family? What would it be like to love someone enough to want all those things with them?

Her heart hurt for Adelaide Draeger. And, maybe a little, for herself.

She blinked, aware that Lam was equally lost in thought, staring at the cakes on the plate, one still in his hand—chocolate melting on his fingers. Whatever he was thinking, he didn't look happy about it.

Poor Lam.

He seemed to be carrying the weight of the world on his broad shoulders. Maybe that's why his smile affected her so much? It was rare. And, because it was rare, it was meant to be treasured.

"This is one of those times," she whispered, hoping to break the tension. "Like Macon said."

He cocked an eyebrow.

"Lost in thought, both of us?" She smiled. "You're thinking she'll like the raspberry cream better."

He blew out a long, slow breath. The corner of his mouth kicked up. "Yup. That's exactly what I was thinking." His words were thick and rough.

"And you're thinking tonight has been...bizarre."

"Going on bizarre night number two for me." His eyebrow rose, and his smile turned a little too irresistible to ignore. "Though I'm thinking tonight's outfit is the most...unforgettable. But it probably wouldn't have made the best first impression."

"At least I'm wearing clothes." Her gaze fell to his very bare, very big, very impressive chest, just long enough for her cheeks to go hot. It was Texas. Summertime. Super hot. And this was his home. He was allowed to sleep without a shirt on—without her staring at his chest. "Guess you don't want that one?"

His gaze fell from her face to his frosting-coated fingers. "I'm eating it. I'm not going to say no to chocolate."

"A man after my own heart." She laughed, leaning forward on her elbows.

"You're not going to sit there and watch, are you?" He frowned.

She smiled. "Um, yes, that was the plan."

He chuckled. "Take one," he encouraged, nodding at the plate.

"Oh, believe me, I taste tested as I went along." She hugged herself, shrugging and shifting in her chair.

"Makes sense." He nodded. "How else would you know if they were any good?"

"Exactly." She pulled her hair over her shoulder. It was a protective habit, like her hair offered up some sort of shield when she was nervous or uncertain. "What?" Why was he looking at her like that? Studying her. And now her cheeks were burning.

"Nothing," he said, but it was something.

She was aware of her ridiculous pajamas, mussed hair, and…always, weight. Try as she might, there was no way to curl up any smaller in her chair.

"Are you cold?" he asked, petit four still in hand.

"No." She forced a smile. "I'm fine. Eat."

He did. One bite and it was gone. Then he was nodding his head, licking his thumb, and smiling ear to ear. "Oh, Gwen, that's good."

There was nothing like getting a compliment on her cooking. It never got old, ever. Nothing delighted her as much as tickling someone's taste buds. "I'm glad you like it."

He reached for another one. "Same thing?"

"Yes." She pushed his hand away. "But try that one next."

His brows rose. "Bossy." But he was grinning.

She laughed. "You fill up on one and you won't appreciate the other flavors."

"What are they?" he asked, eyeing the other cakes.

"Raspberry cream—"

"The one I was thinking about earlier?" He was teasing

her. And enjoying it.

"Yes." She nodded. It would be so easy to get lost in those blue, blue eyes. "Stop interrupting. Raspberry Cream. Peach ginger. And white chocolate."

His gaze swept over her face. "What's your favorite?"

She tore her gaze from his to focus, or try to focus, on the plate of cakes. "That's a tough question. There's something special about each one of them." She pushed the plate closer. "I'm not going to influence your opinion."

Watching Lam devour the sampling she'd made was amusing. He was on the stoic side—until he was eating. With each bite, his features shifted and came to life.

"Food can do that." She shook her head.

"What?" He sat back, stretching his long legs out in front of him.

She decided staring at his bare feet was better than staring at his chest...or stomach. Should a stomach be that hard? "Bring pleasure. Make you happy."

"Is that why you like to cook?" He sounded genuinely interested.

She risked a glance. He looked genuinely interested. "Yes. I like making people happy."

"So far, Gwen, I'd say you know how to make people really happy." He was smiling again, crossing his arms over his chest.

Great. Now she had to avoid staring at his arms, too. Which was pretty impossible. "What about you, Lam?" She stood, carrying his plate to the sink. "What makes you happy?"

He didn't answer.

She glanced up and froze. His face. The pain, raw and devastating, that twisted his features was impossible to miss. He shifted in his chair, resting his elbows on his knees and scrubbing a hand over his face. In that moment, he wasn't a big, intimidating, gorgeous, wall of a man. He was someone hurting. Deeply.

His father? According to her mother, Joseph Draeger had only passed a few months ago. The grief of losing a parent would be unbearable. And here, she'd brought it up—only thinking to ask about his mother's grief, not his. She wiped her hands on a kitchen towel, crossing back to him. There was nothing she could do, but she wasn't one to stand by when someone was hurting.

His shoulder was warm beneath her hand.

At her touch, he looked up. Those beautiful blue eyes were tormented. Haunted. So much grief. And pain. And anger.

It took effort to whisper, "I'm sorry, Lam."

He stood, taking her hand in both of his. Instead of looking at her, he stared at her hand. His thumbs made patterns along her skin, slow—unsteady. Almost timid. And she couldn't take it. She tugged her hand from his and slid her arms around his neck. Hugs were healing, that's what she told her girls. It's what her mother had taught her.

His arms snaked around her waist and tugged her against him, his breath stirred her hair as he buried his face against her neck, and he clung to her. Breath rattled from his chest and one large hand rested at the base of her spine, anchoring them together.

It took time for his hold to loosen and his breathing to

steady but she didn't mind. She could use the hug, too. It had been so long since she'd felt safe in a man's arms. But here, now, she was. She'd stay like this as long as he wanted.

When he did let go, there was no sign of the anguish she'd glimpsed earlier. With his palm pressed to her cheek and those blue eyes boring into hers, there was no misunderstanding what he was thinking. Or what he wanted.

He was going to kiss her. And she wanted him to kiss her. Badly.

"Momma." Jilly Bean's voice was sleep-thick. "Momma?"

He blinked, her daughter's cries snapping them both back to reality. A reality that didn't include the two of them having a late-night rendezvous in the kitchen, wearing next to nothing. Whatever this was, it was most definitely not reality.

"I'm here, Jilly Bean." She hurried to her daughter. "What's up?"

"Bad dreams, Momma." Her little arms twined about Gwen's neck. "You cryin'?"

"No more tears," she whispered.

"You not sad?" One hand twined in her hair. "Momma?"

"No, Jilly Bean, I'm fine. We're good. All of us." She hugged her daughter close, wishing she could chase away the harsh reality of the last few weeks. When Dominic had left, he'd taken everything. She'd had no phone, no food, and no money. And, yes, there'd been more than a handful of nights she'd tried to quiet her tears in her pillow—not always successfully.

"No sad?" Jilly whispered, her little body relaxing against

her mother.

"Nope. We are here with Gramma now."

"Safe and soun'," Jilly said around a yawn.

"Safe and sound, Jilly Bean. I've got you." Gwen risked a look Lam's way. With any luck, he hadn't heard their whispered exchange. "I should get her to bed." She hesitated. "Night, Lam. Sorry if I talked your ear off. Or force fed you."

His nod was stiff. "Gwen." He cleared his throat, his attention settling on Jilly. "You... You're..." He swallowed. "Good night."

Jilly was sound asleep by the time they reached the room they were sharing. She wedged herself between her girls, welcoming their sweet scent and reassuring presence. But, as she was drifting off to sleep, she couldn't help thinking about Lam and what might have happened if Jilly hadn't walked in.

Chapter Five

L AM PLANNED TO skip breakfast. He couldn't face her. Or her girls. Or his family. Or Gwen. Mostly Gwen.

"Get your butt into the kitchen." Macon leaned against the doorframe of the office. "Mom's orders."

He glared at his brother. "I'm not hungry."

"You're being 'rude.'" Macon used air quotes.

"I'm being rude by not being hungry?" He pushed back, hoping like hell his stomach wouldn't start growling.

Macon rolled his eyes. "Don't bite the messenger, bud. Your mother calls, you better answer."

Hearing his father's words from his little brother officially pushed him into a foul mood. The sentiment was sound—respect your mother, always. But he was having a hard time ignoring the hypocrisy. Still, he pushed back his desk chair.

"Kolton's leaving this afternoon, right?" Macon asked.

"Tomorrow morning." He glanced at his brother. "Why?"

"He's a little hard to take this morning. With Gwen." Macon chuckled. "Guess she's fair game and all but—"

"But she's an employee?" Now was not the time to think about last night. Again. Or how close he got to feeling the softness of her lips beneath his. Or how soft the slide of her silky curls had been through his fingers. Or the brush of her breast against his chest…

"What's got you all fired up this morning?" Macon stopped in his tracks.

Lam almost ran into him. There was no way he was going to admit why he was in the state he was in, so he ramped up his scowl.

"Fine." Macon shook his head. "Whatever. Don't tell me." He started walking again. "You ever think you're a little too hardheaded for your own good? That some of us might want to help you? Hell, be here for you?" Macon was the calm one. He wasn't yelling, his voice wasn't raised, but there was a steely edge that told Lam he meant what he was saying. "Yeah, I know. You got it covered." He was walking again, faster this time.

Lam hesitated outside the kitchen door, running a hand through his hair and taking a bracing breath.

Inside was chaos, in the best sense.

His mother was flanked by Jilly and Amy. He hadn't seen her smile like that in months. But she was smiling all right. And eating.

"Chocolate chip pancakes," Tabby said. "They are heaven. You should try them."

"That's why I'm here."

"As you can tell, he gets grumpy when he's hungry." Tabby winked at the girls.

Jilly jumped off her chair and ran over to the kitchen island. "Momma." She waved her mother down to her and whispered something in Gwen's ear.

Seconds later, Jilly was holding a plate stacked high with pancakes. The little girl walked slowly, her tongue sticking out between her lips, as she concentrated on getting the plate to the table. It was close, the entire stack almost wobbling off onto the wooden floors. Jax was more than ready for clean-up duty. But, somehow, she managed to slide the plate onto the table.

"Here go," she said, smiling at him. "No more grump-ies."

He was acutely aware of the fact that he was the center of attention. Kolton and Macon were on the verge of laughter. His mother and Tabby were smitten by the earnest sweetness on Jilly's face. Amy looked worried, like she didn't believe any amount of pancakes had the power to chase away his grumpies.

He did not look at Gwen.

He sat. "Thank you, Jilly. That's mighty kind of you." And took a bite. Heaven. Tabby was right. But then, Gwen had made them.

"Wait, wait." Jilly held up her hand. "This better."

She poured syrup over the stack, and kept on pouring until a pool of syrup was surrounding his pancakes.

"Now." Jilly waited, all smiles.

He eyed the plate, knowing there was only one option. With a resigned sigh, he started eating, ignoring the laughter of his brother and the "ahhs" of his mother and sister. He wasn't done yet. He took a long sip of milk and looked at Amy. "Your mom cooks pretty good, huh, Amy? These are delicious." And he smiled.

Amy's face lit up. "Yup. Momma's best cook evah." She went back to eating.

"Must be. She's got my mom eating, too." He pointed at

his mother with his fork.

"Countin' bites," Amy explained.

Which didn't explain a thing. He made the mistake of looking at Gwen for a clarification. Her hair was twisted up, no sign of the wild curls from the night before. Her apron was blue polka dots over a bright green dress. And her brown eyes? Waiting for him.

"They're learning their numbers. Every bite, the higher the number." She winked.

He swallowed.

"Smart, isn't she?" Kolton chimed in. "So are the girls. What number?"

"Eleven-ty seven," Jilly crowed, climbing back into her chair to spear another bite of pancake.

"That many?" his mother asked. "Goodness, I'm behind."

"How many did you have, Mom?" Macon glanced at her plate. "Not too much, from the looks of it."

"Eat, eat, eat," Jilly encouraged. "Don' wanna waste none." She smiled proudly at her mother.

Lam was smiling, too. How could he not smile at such joyful innocence?

"You were at twelve, I think, Mrs. Draeger." Gwen carried a bowl of fresh strawberries to the table. "Cut a few of these up on top. They'll make it even better. And they were monster bites, Macon. She's eaten more than you think." Her brown eyes darted his way, downright triumphant.

The chocolate chip pancakes were a hit, then. Watching his mother take another bite, the girls declared "twelve-one" loudly, and the laughter that followed made him glad he'd come to breakfast. Correction—been forced to breakfast.

"Strawberries and chocolate." Kolton obligingly scooped up a few and shot Gwen a look that made Lam's insides churn before he started cutting strawberries, all smiles. "Who wants some?"

The girls' hands popped up, and Kolton did a fair job of topping their plates.

"Mrs. Lady needs some," Amy said, pointing at his mother's plate.

Kolton nodded. "Tell me when."

Both girls waited, hands pressed to their mouths, as Kolton kept right on slicing until their mother's plate was covered.

"I think that's enough," Lam interrupted.

The girls were looking at him again. Because he'd barked. Again.

"Cowboy-Man wants some, too," Gwen teased, spooning some of the berries off the top of his mother's plate on to a saucer. "We should share, don't you think?"

"I do," his mother agreed. "Did you know Cowboy-Man is my son? Just like this is your mother."

The girls stared at each other for a long time, then turned to stare at Lam.

"Really?" Amy asked. "Wow."

Macon chuckled.

Tabby looked at him. "I know, right? Poor Mrs. Lady."

Lam almost shot her a look—but the girls were watching, so he didn't. It wasn't easy.

"Here you go." Gwen was standing by his chair, offering him the plate of strawberries.

It didn't seem to matter that she was wearing more clothes. The fact that there were other people in the room didn't help, either. He was just as electrified by her presence as he was last night. Just her, standing there, close enough to him that he could feel her warmth and breathe her in.

"No?" Was it his imagination or did she sound a little breathless? She set the saucer down and went back to the island.

"No wasting," Jilly said in a sing-song voice.

"Yeah, Lam," Kolton agreed. "Especially since Gwen went to all the trouble of getting some for you."

Lam dumped the strawberries onto his pancakes and shoveled a massive bite of syrup, pancakes, and berries into his mouth.

The girls were all wide eyed.

Macon shook his head and did his best not to laugh. And failed.

Tabby didn't even try to hold back. "Lam," she managed to say. "What's gotten into you?"

"Lambert," his mother reprimanded. "You have better manners than that."

He swallowed. "It's so good." Which was true.

"Hear that, Momma?" Amy was so excited. "No more grumpies."

"He's happy." Jilly clapped her hands.

They were staring at him again, he could feel it. But this time, they were all smiling. He couldn't remember the last time he'd made someone smile. It was a sobering realization.

"I think you're right." His mother nodded. "Gwen, maybe you've got something there. Good food feeds a good

71

mood."

"Definitely," Kolton agreed, his attention wandering to Gwen.

Lam bit back a curse. If Kolton wanted to make a fool of himself, he wasn't going to intervene. Unless Gwen was interested. Then, he felt compelled to warn her about his brother's charming ways and wandering eye.

She didn't seem to notice Kolton. Her attention bounced between her girls and his mother and the food she was chopping. She moved with a fluid ease. Confident. But then, this was her passion, as was evidenced by the incredible food on his plate and in his stomach.

A booted foot landed a solid kick to his shin, jarring him.

Tabby was studying him. "You've got something, right there." She pointed at the corner of her mouth.

When he pressed his napkin to his mouth, there was nothing there. Because his sister had caught him staring at Gwen—and she was messing with him. "Very funny."

She laughed. "I'm not sure it's funny. But it's about to get...entertaining around here."

"What?" Macon asked. "What did I miss?"

"Nothing." He stood, taking care to sound calm—not irritated. It was a challenge. "Nothing at all." He carried his plate from the table, rinsing the remaining syrup residue, and turning to load it in the dishwasher.

Gwen kept right on chopping, her brown eyes following his every movement. "Thank you, Cowboy-Man."

He mumbled something and left, hoping like hell he could come up with some excuse to skip lunch—and further opportunity to make an ass of himself.

GWEN SWATTED A fly away and gently turned the tomato on its stem until it came free. In her basket, she had five ruby-red tomatoes, two yellow onions, some yellow squash, and three smallish cucumbers. While she was exploring dinner options, the girls were running around the kitchen garden, stooping to explore bugs, or poking at an unknown vegetable until she told them what it was. So far, she'd been lucky with her girls—they'd eat anything. From brussels sprouts to bologna, if she served it, they ate it.

"Momma." Jilly came running up. "Was' this?"

Gwen turned. "It's a grasshopper." She frowned. "They're here to steal all the vegetables."

Jilly held up the large brown-and-green bug and stared it in the eye. "No stealing, Mr. Grasshopper."

The grasshopper leapt from her hand, prompting an ear-curdling scream from Jilly and sending Amy, running to her side.

"Jilly?" Amy asked, wide-eyed and nervous.

"Silly Jilly." Gwen hugged her girls close. "Did that grasshopper scare you?" They nodded. "That's what they do. They hop."

"Like a fwog?" Amy asked.

"An' a kangaroo?" Jilly asked.

"Yes." She tapped them each on the nose. "Only small-er." With their bulging eyes and unpredictable leaps, she'd always thought grasshoppers were funny critters. When she'd been little, she'd hopped around the garden while her mother picked veggies for the evening meal.

The girls were smiling now, sifting through her basket.

"What should we make for dinner?" she asked. "I thought we could grill the veggies? And some chicken?"

"Stick fish," Amy suggested. "Cowboy-Man'll like it."

The idea of Lam Draeger eating fish sticks was too hard to conjure, but she decided not to argue with her daughter. "I'm not sure I put enough on the grocery list, Amy. We'll have to check when Gramma gets back."

Her mother had offered to take the girls into town with her for her weekly shop, but Gwen had been uneasy about letting them go. She and Dominic's last fight had left a lingering fear. He'd thrown her total reliance on him in her face, adding that the girls would be better off with him, and, if he ever left, he threatened to come for them once he was settled. The likelihood of him following through on his threat? Slim…but he'd planted a seed and it had taken root.

Keeping the girls by her side had hurt her mother, she could tell, but she didn't want to share her fears. Or worry her over nothing. Still…did she wish she could go back so her mother was a part of their lives from the beginning? Yes. It was one of the many mistakes she'd made over the last four years. But wasting time regretting what could have been wouldn't change a thing. They were here now, already in love with their gramma. The three of them would be inseparable in no time.

"Look, Momma," Amy's voice turned soft and excited, her little hands clasped in front of her.

She turned to see Jax coming down the garden path. And where Jax was—if he wasn't with Amy—Lam would be, too. But that was not the reason she was smoothing her hair or wiping her hands off on her apron.

"Jax," Amy whispered, her grin so big, it was a wonder her little girl didn't explode with excitement.

"You've made a good friend, haven't you?" She watched the dog circle her daughter before sidling close to sniff and lick her cheek. If her daughter was enamored, the feeling was mutual. "You're a good boy, Jax."

"Good good good boy." Amy's near-reverential tone was too much.

She laughed. "That good, huh?"

"Momma, this?" Jilly asked, holding up her hand.

Lam came around the end of the shed. A fine coating of white dust covered his well-worn jeans. His straw hat, one that had seen better days, sat low on his forehead. Prettiful. That's what Amy had said about Jax. Well, that was exactly how she felt about Lam.

"Momma?" Jilly repeated, ending her perusal of Lam. Her boss. Her hot cowboy-man boss. "See?"

Gwen saw. It was a large red ant, walking in a circle on Jilly's little hand before starting up her arm.

"That's a fire ant." Lam reached over her shoulder to swipe the bug from Jilly's arm. "They'll bite you, Jilly. You see them, you stay away, okay?"

Fire ants were bad news. One or two bites stung. More than that? It could make a person, especially a small someone, seriously ill.

"They can make you sick, sweetie. Mr…Cowboy-Man is right. Okay, Jilly?" she repeated, wanting her curious daughter to understand how important this was.

"Yes, Momma." Her big eyes looked beyond her to Lam.

Lam was standing right behind her, close. So close that if she turned, she'd be nose-to-nose with him. Because he was protecting Jilly. She sighed and stepped forward and away from Lam. "What do you want the girls to call you?" Cowboy-Man didn't imply the level of respect and separation she wanted to develop between them. This wistful daydreaming about Lam had to stop.

When he didn't answer, she glanced his way.

He was squatting between the girls, holding a peach. "It's soft."

Both girls obligingly stroked the fruit.

"Smells good, too," he said, sniffing it.

Both girls followed suit.

"And it tastes better than candy." He was smiling. "I bet, with some of your mom's ice cream, there's nothing better in the whole wide world." Those blue eyes bounced from her to the fruit, his jaw muscle tightening. Like last night. When his hand rested against her cheek…

What was he thinking?

"You know what Cowboy-Man is thinking?" she asked.

Three pair of eyes, four—Jax was listening, too—turned her way.

"It's snack time." She reached for the peach, the brush of his fingertips against hers quick—but potent. A spark. Like a static electricity shock. Only a hundred times stronger. From the way he was rubbing his thumb against his forefingers, she knew she hadn't imagined it.

"Snack?" Jilly asked, her excitement contagious.

"Yum," Amy added.

"What are we having?" Lam asked, standing to stare

down at her.

She swallowed. "You already said it. Ice cream and peaches. If you think you can get a few more of these?"

"I think I might locate one or two or a dozen…in the orchard." He chuckled. "If you three want to help us get them?"

"Yes," Amy nodded, patting Jax. "Good at helpin'."

"Me too, me too." Jilly jumped up and down. "I'm a grasshop."

"A mighty fine little grasshopper, too." Lam just kept right on smiling.

It wasn't that she preferred the somber, scowling Lam, but that the somber, scowling Lam was easier to keep at arm's length. This Lam, with his smiles and conversation and interest in her girls, was far too appealing. And tempting. *Going off on a peach-picking expedition together makes perfect sense.*

"Can we, Momma?" Jilly asked, still hopping.

"Peez." Amy had her arms around Jax's neck, waiting.

Lam tipped back his hat, a dark curl falling onto his forehead, his blue gaze meeting hers.

Even Jax seemed to be waiting for her answer, ears perked up, eyes on her face. Like she could disappoint them? "I guess so."

Jilly took Lam's hand like it was the most natural thing in the world.

And there it was again, that lightning-fast shift of emotions on his face. Not so fast that she missed his grief and misery and pain that had him twisted up inside though. When he smiled down at Jilly, squeezing her little hand in his, his smile was in place.

Amy and Jax followed. If Jax had hands, Gwen had no doubt the dog would be holding on to Amy. As it was, he stayed right by her side, giving her hand a head-butt or lick—and delighting Amy to no end.

In three days, her entire world had changed. She didn't have to worry about the girls having empty tummies or how they'd manage to make ends meet. She did have to worry about how quickly her daughters were attaching themselves to the Draegers, though. This was a temporary arrangement, period. Once she'd saved up some money and found the right job, she and the girls would start over. She might not exactly know what she wanted, but she knew exactly what she didn't want: having to rely on someone else. She'd had dreams, she just had to remember them. And once she did, incredible gardens, state-of-the-art kitchens, cute dogs, and gorgeous, broody cowboy-men weren't going to stand in her way.

Chapter Six

NOTHING LIKE HEADING inside for a conference call to negotiate the breeding contract of a two-hundred-thousand-dollar-earning bull and getting waylaid by a toddler holding a fire ant. But, dammit, it was a fire ant and Jilly was tiny. If she'd found one fire ant, she'd find more. The image of her covered in welts grabbed hold of him so fast, he'd had no choice but to keep an eye on her. That's how he'd wound up in the peach orchard, Gwen's daughters taking turns riding on his shoulders, to pick peaches. And missed his conference call.

He'd gone from being dusty and tired to being dusty, sticky—thanks to the girls' peach-covered fingers—and, now that they were back in the safe confines of the house, strangely relaxed. Gwen was a hands-on sort of mother. It was the girls who washed the fruit and, once they were peeled and sliced, it was the girls who added butter, cinnamon, and sugar before Gwen put the pan in the oven. While they waited, they worked together to scrape all the peels and pits into the trash, scrub down the cutting board, and remove any sticky pulp that might attract ants.

"Smells ready," Gwen announced, cracking the oven enough to peer inside.

The glorious scent filled the kitchen, making his taste

buds ache.

"Yay!" The girls jumped up and down in excitement.

He chuckled, their unabashed enthusiasm impossible to resist.

Gwen shot him a quick grin. "Guess my girls are just as enamored with food as I am?" Her smile wavered then. He'd seen that before—a chink in her confidence. While he didn't know who or what triggered it, he'd like to find out—just so he could give them a kick in the butt. "Sit at the table, girlies. I'll get you some."

The girls ran to the table and scrambled into chairs.

Damn it all, he was smiling again.

"Here you go," Gwen pressed a large bowl into his hands. "Today was a treat."

He nodded before he could stop himself.

Her grin was worth it.

"Cowboy-Man, come sit," Jilly called, patting the table beside him.

"Jilly. Manners," Gwen reprimanded.

Jilly nodded. "Sit, peez, Cowboy-Man?"

Honestly? At the moment, something bordering panic was setting it. The innocent expectation on Jilly and Amy's faces tore at wounds he couldn't face.

"Pretty peez," Amy added.

He sat.

"What's cooking?" Kolton and Macon pushed through the kitchen door and came to a screeching halt.

Yes, he was wearing one of Marta's aprons—the girls in-sisted. It was nothing special. Just a plain blue apron, no bows or ruffles...only one butterfly on the pocket. But, considering the amount of dust on his clothes, it had seemed necessary. Then.

Now?

He didn't miss the way Macon nudged Kolton, the surprise on Kolton's face, or the way his jaw set.

Great, just great. The two of them had enough problems without adding some nonexistent rivalry for Gwen. Did he like the idea of Kolton blatantly pursuing Gwen? No. But it wasn't because he wanted her. And he didn't appreciate that his brothers were immediately jumping to that conclusion.

"Enjoying yourself?" Kolton's gaze narrowed, his smile too forced to be real.

"Peaches." Jilly took the bowl from Gwen.

"Ice cream." Amy frowned as her ice cream slipped off her spoon and onto the scoured wooden-table top.

"Hold up." Without thinking, Lam wiped the dollop of melting ice cream up and put a spoonful from his bowl into hers.

"He's sharing his ice cream," Macon whispered—but it wasn't a real whisper. He was loud enough that everyone heard and could interpret whatever they wanted.

"There's plenty," Gwen offered. If she picked up on Macon's teasing, there was no sign of it. But then, she knew there was some truth to the teasing. There was no denying what had almost happened last night. She hadn't said a thing today, and he was thankful, but every accidental touch was a jolt to the system—a fact she was just as aware of as he was.

"Are you kidding?" Kolton leaned against the kitchen island, giving her a long lingering look. "There's no way I'm saying no to something that smells this good."

"Thanks, Gwen." Macon smiled. "Guess you all found the orchard?"

"Cowboy-Man held us up up up." Jilly held her spoon up high.

"He's tall." Amy drew out the 'l' in tall, then giggled.

Kolton and Macon exchanged another look. Dammit.

"When are you heading out, Kolton?" He finished off his bowl of ice cream, savoring the last bite of peaches and cinnamon. "I figure it'll take you a week or so to get there and back—with the trailer and all."

Kolton tapped his spoon against his bowl, eyebrows high. "A week? I could probably cut that down." He gave Gwen another smile.

Lam sighed. "When you're done with your snack, why don't you two come see me in the office." It wasn't a question.

"Cowboy-Man hungry-grumpy?" Amy whispered.

"Sad?" Jilly shrugged. "Peaches gone."

Instantly, he kicked himself. Kolton was acting like an idiot, but he didn't have to respond. Without realizing it, he'd snapped—again—and the girls had noticed. For being so small and cute, they were remarkably intuitive. God knows his son had been the same. Grant had liked to make people happy—telling silly jokes and giving hugs at just the right time. His boy had given the best hugs.

He swallowed, closing his eyes against the memories that threatened to swallow him whole.

Kolton. He was a piece of work. What to do about his brother? He was sweet on Gwen. Understood. But, knowing his brother, it wouldn't last long. What *would* last long? The money they'd get from selling and delivering the bull on time. Because it was Kolton's job to help him keep this place up and running. Anything, or anyone, that would get in the way with that was a problem.

Gwen. He wasn't going there.

He sighed.

With any luck, Kolton would get over Gwen by the time he got back to Last Stand. If he was really lucky, his brother would meet someone else. Someone who wasn't Gwen.

Dammit.

"All done?" Gwen was standing beside his chair.

Her hair was slipping free, a tumble of wild red-gold curls. If his brothers hadn't been in the room, he'd have smiled up at her, letting himself appreciate the color in her cheeks and the mingling scent of peaches, cinnamon, and sweetness that clung to her. As it was, he nodded and tried not to stare. Or frown. "Thank you."

She smiled. "Thank *you*. The girls and I enjoyed it."

If his brothers hadn't been there, he'd probably have offered to take them again or something along those lines. Instead he nodded.

"I'd be glad to take you peach picking anytime you want," Kolton said. "You girls up for it?"

Amy and Jilly shrugged, their enthusiasm dimming, and their eyelids drooping.

"Naptime," Gwen's voice was low. "After all that hard work, they should sleep well. Just leave the plates, and I'll clean up when I get back." With a smile, she steered the girls out the rear of the kitchen, down the hall that led to Marta's small apartment.

"What's the problem?" Kolton asked the minute the door swung shut.

Lam didn't say anything. He knew Kolton. He didn't really want an answer. But Macon tried anyway.

"She works here, Kolt. And, honestly, it sounds like she's been through some stuff. Maybe—"

"What the hell does that mean?" Kolton swelled up.

"You've known her, what, two days?" Macon shook his head. "Dial it back a little."

"I'm not the one using her kids to get to her—"

"You done?" Lam cut him off. "Delivering this bull is serious business. We've been negotiating for three weeks. I expect it to get done. And done right. Not shortcuts." He paused. "Your social life is your business—as long as it doesn't interfere with the family business. Understood?"

Kolton's face turned dark red. "You sound just like him right now."

He didn't have to ask who Kolton was talking about. He knew. It was no secret that his relationship with their father had been contentious. Kolton's dig was a kick to the chest.

Macon groaned. "Kolton. Don't be such a di—"

The back door opened and Marta came in, arms loaded with shopping bags. "Boys. Glad you're here. I could use some help unloading the truck." Her voice tapered off as she sized up the room. "You three going at it again?" She shook her head. "Not in my kitchen. Go on, now. Make yourselves useful."

GWEN DIDN'T SEE Lam for three days.

Kolton had gone "on a job," Macon was called to do fireman things, and Tabby managed to book another wedding for the ranch, so things were pretty quiet. Except for Mrs. Draeger, her mother, and the girls, she didn't have much company.

What was Lam up to? She had no idea. And since it wasn't her place to ask, it remained a mystery until Jilly did what precocious three-year-olds tended to do.

"Mrs. Lady?" Jilly poked at her biscuit. "Is Cowboy-Man gone?"

Mrs. Draeger reached for one of Gwen's fluffy butter-milk biscuits. "What do you mean 'gone'?"

Jilly shrugged, momentarily distracted as her gramma spread a thick layer of raspberry jam on her biscuit. "Daddy left. Cowboy-Man, too?"

Gwen was horrified.

What Jilly had said was absolutely true but...it was her business. And embarrassing. The sympathy now lining Adelaide Draeger's face made it doubly so.

"Jilly Bean, eat your breakfast, please." She nudged her daughter's jam-laden biscuit closer. "Cowboy-Man is busy working somewhere."

"No eat, gets grumpy." Amy shook her head. "Poor Cowboy-Man."

Which made them all laugh.

Her daughter had a point. What had Lam been eating for the last three days? Other than the late-night snacks she'd left him? He worked hard, he had to be building up an appetite.

"You know something, girls?" Mrs. Draeger reached for the chocolate-hazelnut spread. "I'll make sure Cowboy-Man comes to dinner."

"Jax-y, too?" Amy asked, licking some honey off one of her fingers.

Mrs. Draeger nodded. "I'm sure Jax is missing you, too."

Amy smiled.

"It's not like Lambert Draeger to miss a meal. Not ever." Her mother sounded off. "You can always set your clock by that boy for breakfast, lunch, and dinner."

"He works too hard." Mrs. Draeger shook her head. "I understand. I'd rather he drowned his sorrows in his work than, say, drink. But he's too young to stop really living."

"He and his father must have been very close." She winced, realizing Lam's father was Mrs. Draeger's beloved spouse.

"Oh, those two butted heads more than I liked. They tried to hide it from me. But I could tell. So could Marta." Mrs. Draeger smiled up at her mother. "We women always know these things."

Marta nodded. "Stubborn fools, the lot of them. The day before Kolton left, he and Lam were bowed up at each other in the kitchen."

Which was news to Gwen. And Mrs. Draeger too.

"Those boys wear me out." Mrs. Draeger sighed, setting her half-eaten biscuit aside. "The last years have been too hard to let little irritations wear at what's left of our family. Lam...well, he's been eaten up inside for so long, I wonder if he'll ever get over it."

Her mother took and squeezed Adelaide Draeger's hand.

"He'll sort it out, Addy. That sort of hurt takes time to heal. If it ever really does."

Gwen suspected they were talking about more than just Mr. Draeger's death, but didn't feel it was her place to ask questions—especially about personal matters. Privacy was to be valued, she understood that. She'd been so absorbed in settling in and creating a routine for the girls to consider what had been happening on the ranch in the years since she'd left. Clearly, there was a lot she didn't know.

"He sad," Jilly said.

"Who, Jilly?" Gwen asked.

"Cowboy-Man," Amy answered.

"You're right." Mrs. Draeger nodded, her gaze lingering on Amy, then Jilly. "And I think I know why he's been so scarce recently." She sighed.

Gwen bit her lip, so many questions bouncing around in her mind. She settled on, "How about we make him something special for dinner? Is there something he likes? Other than chicken fried steak?"

Mrs. Draeger took another bite of her chocolate-covered biscuit, looking thoughtful as she chewed.

"Pot roast," her mother said.

Mrs. Draeger nodded.

Because Lam Draeger was a meat and potatoes man. Not that he'd rejected any of the treats she'd left him. Crème brûlée. A chocolate parfait. A strawberry layer cake with whipped cream and preserves. And, she'd noticed, her homemade ice cream was almost gone.

"Pot roast, it is." She nodded. "Dessert?"

Mrs. Draeger nodded and looked at them. "A plain white

cake with chocolate icing. It's been his favorite since he was a boy."

Gwen tried not to be too deflated by the uncomplicated meal selection. All she could do was make the very best pot roast and white cake with chocolate icing in the whole world.

And hours later, she was pretty sure she'd succeeded and still had time to change for dinner. If she took a little extra time, it had nothing to do with seeing Lam and everything to do with…okay, it had something to do with Lam.

As much as she didn't want to admit it, she'd missed his company.

The girls set the table. Her mother filled the glasses with iced tea for the adults and fresh peach lemonade for the girls. Mrs. Draeger cut the still-warm bread and put it on a platter. And Gwen was doing her best not to notice that it was after six thirty. Then sixty forty. At seven, she went ahead and served the girls dinner.

When it was clear Lam wasn't coming, Mrs. Draeger said good night, and her mother took the girls to bed while she cleaned up the kitchen.

She had no right to be angry. If Lam Draeger didn't want to eat her cooking, that was his prerogative. He'd never said he would. But…well, the girls were disappointed. And the food? She'd made a lot. Did she make him a plate and leave it for his midnight snack? Or did she put everything away and leave him to fend for himself?

It would serve him right.

He knew when dinner was. His mother had gone out of her way to specifically request his presence. But he'd chosen not to come.

She couldn't help but feel responsible. Was he avoiding her?

He was going hungry and slinking around the house—granted it was a huge house—because of her?

That couldn't be true, could it? There was only one way to find out. Ask him herself.

Chapter Seven

L AM FINISHED THE forecasting model for the new breeding program, signed off on the revamped contracts with the feed supplier, and set up a few appointments with breeding specialists—anything to avoid looking at the information the private investigator had delivered today. Now that he had answers, did he really want them? He'd sliced open the envelope with his letter opener, but couldn't bring himself to look. Once he did, there would be no way to unlearn the information he'd find there.

Jax jumped up from his mat in the corner, whimpering once, his ears perking up, to stare at the door. There was a knock. It wasn't entirely unexpected, considering he'd missed dinner.

"Come in," he called out.

The door opened, and Gwen came in, carrying a tray. Gwen, with her long hair down and her fuzzy-sock-covered feet. She was the last person he'd expected—the last person he wanted to see. Which was a bald-faced lie. He'd missed seeing her. Missed seeing the girls. It had taken a concerted effort to steer clear of the kitchen until after ten.

After that, he'd wander in, hoping she'd be there. She never was. But there'd been snacks and, last night, a picture from the girls. It was a unicorn color sheet, streaked heavily with purple and pink and silver. One of them had drawn what looked to him like a cowboy hat. Since he knew he couldn't tack it to the corkboard that lined most of his office, he tucked it into his desk drawer.

He waited, hoping the girls were with her. Being alone with her always scrambled things up inside. He rubbed his hands on his jeans, his eyes pinned on the door. No girls. No backup. Just Gwen. His heart thumped.

Her brown gaze flicked his way before taking in his office, still holding a tray piled high. He stood, ready to take it from her.

She ignored him and set the tray on the coffee table. "I brought you dinner."

Dammit. "You didn't have to—"

"I did." She faced him, crossing her arms over her chest. "The girls insisted."

He smiled.

She shook her head, sighing. "Your mother was really disappointed you weren't at dinner. She'd counted on you being there." A nod toward the plate on the tray.

Pot roast, potatoes and carrots, a side salad, and a massive slice of white cake with thick chocolate frosting. All his favorites. He frowned.

His mother had laid the guilt on thick. Everything from how lonely she was, to little Jilly worrying he'd disappeared. He knew good and well his mother wasn't alone. She had Gwen, the girls, and Marta to keep her company. Why would he want to eat with a passel of women and girls? He shouldn't. And he wasn't about to admit otherwise.

"Amy said you must be super grumpy because you ha-

ven't eaten. She wanted me to feed you—to cheer you up."
She swallowed. "I told her I'd try. I'm not holding out much
hope—I'm a realist." Her gaze locked with his. "I'm curious,
though. My mother said you never, ever missed a meal.
Before."

He was trapped then, defenseless against the power of
her chocolate-brown gaze. He hadn't meant to upset the
girls. He hadn't meant to upset anyone. He was pretty sure
he didn't have that sort of power.

"Before us, I mean. Though I'm pretty sure you knew
that." Her voice lowered. "Is it my girls? We don't have to
eat with the family. It wasn't my idea—it was your mom's
and Tabby's. But I get it. We're not family. And they, the
girls, can be a handful. I know."

She was wrong. Her girls brought joy back. When they
were around, it felt wrong not to smile and enjoy the little
things. But having them here was also a reminder of everything he'd had. And lost. Not that Amy or Jilly were
responsible for that. "They're fine." He ground out the
words, running a hand over his face.

"Then it's me?" Her brows rose.

Yes. He swallowed. This was dangerous territory. "Gwen,
I'm not sure what you're after here?"

Her eyes widened. "You don't?"

He knew that she knew he was hiding out—from her.
But he wasn't going to admit that either. "No, ma'am."

The corner of her mouth twitched. "Meaning you have a
perfectly good explanation for skipping every meal for the
last three days?"

He crossed his arms over his chest, hoping a scowl and

silence would end this conversation. And she'd go. His hands fisted.

He didn't want her to go.

She stepped forward, red staining her cheeks. "Your mother is worried about you." Her eyes blazed. "But she's grieving, too, Lam. You lost your father, she lost her husband. I know you all have lives and jobs, but carving out time for meals—even one—might take the edge off both of your grief. Because, whether you want to face it, you're grieving too. You should. You've lost your father."

He missed his father. But he grieved—*ached*—for his son. She might not know that—he didn't know what she'd been told, but chances were his family had told her more than he'd want her to know. If not, well that was fine. She didn't need to know that.

And, right now, with her fired up and in his space, he didn't want to think about grief or his family or how she'd knocked his world off its axis or how he was beginning to seriously question staying away from her. Her temper was mesmerizing.

She was beautiful. Damn beautiful. And as she stepped closer, poking him in the chest, he was glad she'd come into his office to give him a talking-to.

"You not being there for her? I don't want to be the reason for that." Her voice wobbled. "If my being around bothers you—"

"Bothers me?" Was she kidding? Didn't she understand? He had to stay away. If he didn't? "That's not the right word. And you know it."

Her brown eyes widened, and her cheeks turned a pretty

pink.

He blew out a deep breath and reached for her. No more thinking or talking or resisting. No more. Just this—kissing her. Soft. Light. Cradling her face with his hands. Sealing his lips to hers. It was what needed to happen—what he needed to do. Pure instinct. Natural.

Was it a shock? Hell yes. But she felt so good in his arms. So damn good. His lips lingered, savored, and once she swayed into him, he was done for. The feel of her melting against him and the slide of her hands up and around his neck had him running his fingers through the silky curls of her hair to cup the back of her head. Kissing her was everything he knew it would be.

And when he let go, he knew it could never happen again.

He stepped back, scraping a hand over his face. No point pretending now. "That's why." He risked looking at her. And bit back a curse.

Her hair was mussed, thanks to him. Her full lips parted. And her brown eyes? They were burning with a different kind of fire. "You... But..."

He tore his gaze away. There wasn't much to say. He'd no right to kiss her. No right to touch her. "Thanks for dinner."

"Lam." It was a whisper.

He looked at her, bracing himself. Now she really had a reason to chew him out.

"What if I said I'd hoped you'd do that?" She swallowed. "Not now, though. I'm mad at you now. At least, I was." She blinked rapidly, stumbling over her words. "But before, I mean, I have thought about that—kissing you. Even though we both know it's not a good idea."

He should be relieved. She wasn't mad—hell, she agreed with him. About wanting to be kissed and knowing it was wrong. But he wasn't relieved. He was…disappointed. "It is. Really bad." He nodded, trying his hardest not to get distracted by the way she was nibbling the inside of her lower lip.

She nodded, pulling her hair over one shoulder. He didn't know what the look on her face was. She seemed to be mulling something over. Something about him. She was staring at him mighty hard. In a way that made his heart thud all over again. "But…" Her teeth sank into her lip.

"But?" No. No buts. It was a bad idea. So was moving closer to her, so close he could see the freckles on the bridge of her nose. Now he was holding his breath like a damn teenager, hoping, and waiting to see what she said next.

She was kissing him this time, her arms sliding around his waist, her hands twisting in the fabric of his shirt, and her chest crushed against his. The feel of her was too much, crashing into his senses and stealing his ability to think about all the reasons this was a very bad idea.

When their lips parted and their tongues touched, he was pretty sure this was the best idea he'd ever had. Rather, she'd had—since she was the one kissing him. But now that she was, he was going to make damn sure she knew exactly how much he wanted her.

His hands slid up her back, beneath her hair, along her neck, to cradle her cheeks once more. She leaned into his palm, her hold on his shirt tightening. His lips moved along her cheek to her temple, lingering long enough to trace his nose along her ear, and brush his lips against the skin beside her ear. She shuddered, arching into him, wanting his touch.

Being responsible for her reaction—sigh and moan and gasp—was both empowering and humbling. It had been so long since he'd wanted a woman, he'd forgotten what it was to have one want him back.

A sudden crash had him pushing her behind him...until he realized what had happened. Jax stood, a dinner roll hanging out of his mouth, a broken bread plate and rolls scattered all over the wooden floorboards. His dog had no idea what that damn roll had cost him.

But he did. His arms had never felt so empty.

She laughed, breathless, and slipped around him. "Were you hungry?" She knelt, picking up the pieces. "Lam's been feeding you, I hope?"

"Every day, two times a day." Five seconds ago, he'd had her in his arms, now she was worrying about the dog? Maybe that kiss hadn't shaken her to the core the way it had him.

But he saw the tremor in her hand as she reached for Jax and, dammit, it made him happy. "He's been eating better than I have."

"Whose choice was that?" When her gaze bounced his way, her cheeks blossomed red all over again.

She had a point. If the dog had been eating better than he had, it was because of his self-imposed exile. Other than the late-night surprises Gwen had left for him, he'd been living on the less-than-healthy snacks and frozen meals he and his brothers kept in the main barn because Marta refused to have the stuff in her kitchen. He didn't say anything, but his expression had her laughing.

"Maybe Amy's right and he is grumpy hungry?" She pretend-whispered to Jax. But the teasing was cut short when she dropped the china in her hand, flinching, before sticking her finger in her mouth.

"Careful." Lam knelt beside her and took her hand in his, holding it up for inspection.

"I'm fine." She tried to pull away.

"Let me see." He held on to her hand. Soft skin under his rough touch.

"Yes, sir," she murmured, shooting him a look.

"I think I've seen Amy do that a time or two." Teasing. Distracting. Inspecting the cut was better than getting caught up in those brown eyes again. Especially this close. Close enough to lean in for another kiss. His gaze shifted to her lips.

"What?" Her voice was low—husky.

"That look." He cleared his throat and grinned, dabbing away the blood on her fingertip. "Doesn't look like there's anything in it. I think you'll survive."

She sat back, chewing on her lip again.

He wasn't sure he'd ever be able to look at her without thinking of that kiss—and the way she'd come alive in his arms. Right now, it was all he could think about. With her hair falling over one shoulder and her gaze fixed on his face, the urge to pick up right where they'd left off was overwhelming.

Jax nudged him with his nose. Until now, he'd never realized how terrible the dog's timing was. Or not. Jax was probably saving him from making an even bigger mistake.

One kiss was just—fine, a couple of kisses—were nothing to worry about.

Were they? No. They weren't.

Who was he kidding? He wasn't sure what to make of what had just happened.

To him, there was a whole lot more going on than just a kiss. But that was him. And he'd gone without for a long time.

Since he'd become a master at avoiding his emotions, he pushed aside any further analysis of this evening's odd turn. Instead, he chuckled, ran a hand over the dog's head, and did his best to diffuse the crackling tension pulling them together. "You get lost in thought again?" She was so damn pretty.

An unsteady breath slipped between her lips, and she blinked rapidly, her gaze flitting across his face before she said, "I know what you're thinking." She smiled.

"I can't wait to hear this." After making sure there was no shards of china on the floor, he sat, stretching his legs out before him, and reached for his dinner plate and silverware. "Go on."

"You were just about to give me your word you'll be in the kitchen for breakfast tomorrow." She cocked her head to one side, eyebrows arched. "And you're looking forward to my French toast and a bacon breakfast casserole. Am I right?"

She was back to that—needling him about meals. He was thinking about kissing and touching and holding on to her, and she was thinking about how bad a son he was. Not that she was wrong. Pretty much everything she'd said was right. His mother did need the company and support of her kids. He needed to remember that and not let this bizarre connection with Gwen get in the way. But he kept on chewing, his taste buds too happy for him to answer.

She reached for his dinner plate, her brows high. "Right?"

"Fine." He swallowed, holding the plate away from her. "But only if you use a pound of bacon."

"Fine." She pushed off the floor. "I'll leave you to enjoy your dinner in peace and get back to work. See you tomorrow." She was gone before he had a chance to think of a reason to ask her to stay.

GWEN WAS PLEASED with her morning's efforts. A breakfast feast, to be sure. Perfectly battered French toast, warmed maple syrup, homemade chocolate-hazelnut spread, a bacon-heavy breakfast casserole, and a berry salad with fresh whipped cream.

Amy and Jilly sat, wearing their favorite fairy princess dresses and tiny glitter wings, at the end of the table. They'd decided to use their best manners so Cowboy-Man wouldn't get grumpy. She'd tried to assure them that Cowboy-Man had a lot of work to do and he wasn't grumpy so much as a serious grown-up man, but her girls weren't convinced.

"Who are these gorgeous creatures?" Tabby asked, pressing a hand to her chest. "Be still my heart. You two are the most beautiful fairy princesses on Draeger Ranch."

Amy smiled. "Thank you."

"Are there more?" Jilly's brow dipped into a furrow.

Tabby laughed. "I'm not sure."

Her mother tapped her chin, as if she were thinking hard. "Maybe we can go looking for fairies later this afternoon?"

"Can we, Momma?" Jilly asked.

"Jax, too?" Amy turned pleading eyes her way.

Amy was a little too fond of Lam's dog. "Jax is Cowboy-Man's dog, Amy. He's a working animal. He has to earn his keep." She added the butter dish to the table and nodded. "What do you think? Look good?"

Jilly held up her thumb. Amy held up both thumbs.

"Lovely, Gwen." Her mother nodded. "The food and the table."

"I can't really top what they said." Tabby pointed at the girls. "But, if it tastes as good as it looks, I'm going to have to put on my stretchy pants. I have a meeting with a bride and her mother later on. Thank goodness, she's not a bridezilla."

"Was' that?" Amy asked.

"Monster?" Jilly asked.

"They can be." Tabby grinned, then paused and looked at Gwen. "Can I ask a question? It's an idea. One you can totally say no to—"

"Ask away." Gwen waited, beyond curious.

"You know the ranch does some events here, weddings and reunions and parties and the like? Up until now, it's up to the guest to take care of food...*but* I was thinking, if you were interested, it might be something you could do? We get some pretty big spenders, from all over, and you'd have a chance to cook all sorts of fancy stuff." She paused.

"Oh, Gwen, that would be perfect," her mother gushed.

"You could stay here. With the girls. I'd love that, Gwen. You know I'd love to be a regular part of their lives. And yours. I've missed you so much." Her mother gave her a quick squeeze. "I would love for you and the girls to move here, with me, forever. No pressure, though."

Gwen chuckled. She wanted her mother to be a regular part of the girls' lives, too. Wanted them to have a home. But she'd never imagined winding up in Last Stand for good.

"Just think about it, okay?" Tabby shrugged. "Don't answer right away."

"Answer what?" Mrs. Draeger came into the kitchen. "Oh gracious, I get to have breakfast with fairies and eat like a king."

"A queen." Jilly was all smiles. "Need a crown."

"I'll have to find it after breakfast." Mrs. Draeger sat at the end of the table. "Just us girls?"

"Nope." Macon peaked in. "If there's enough for me?" His smile grew as he assessed the table. "There's enough for me."

"Maybe." Lam pushed past him, looking big and manly and gorgeous enough to make her a tiny bit breathless. "But I'm really hungry." He eyed the table and started making his plate. "Really, really hungry. You might have to make some more, Gwen."

Amy and Jilly's gaze shifted from the food piled high to Lam.

"Wow," Amy whispered.

"That's *really* hungry," Jilly added.

Lam sat and nodded. "Yes, indeed-y."

Gwen was struck by the way his gaze lingered on her

girls. There was a fleeting tenderness on his face. And a yearning. She'd been so busy settling in and fighting her out-of-control attraction to get to know Lam—the real Lam. Not the overwhelmingly handsome man who had her weak-kneed and clinging to him the night before, but the successful, business-minded man, who worked hard to care for his family. The day-in, day-out Lam. She wanted to know this man. And that made her anxious.

"Looks good, Gwen." Macon sat. "Food at the station can't compare."

"Of course it can't. Gwen's a chef." Her mother smiled at her. "Trained in a fancy school. Worked under the best chefs." The pride in her mother's voice warmed her heart.

Dominic had been an incredible chef. Passionate, creative, and inspiring. The same couldn't be said of his relationships. They'd started with a flame but quickly turned to ashes. Her career had suffered terribly, but she'd ended up with the girls so, in the end—jobless, near-homeless and completely broke—she'd still come out the winner.

"You can tell," Tabby said.

"You can." Mrs. Draeger nodded. "What were you two talking about when I came in? What does Gwen need to think about?"

"Momma cookin'." Amy watched as her mother cut up her French toast.

"Us stayin'." Jilly popped a strawberry into her mouth.

"Well, I like the sound of that." Mrs. Draeger nodded. "It's been too quiet and sad since…" She stopped. "Well, for a while now."

Since her husband's passing. That made sense, of course.

But, if that was what she was talking about, why were Macon and Tabby and Mrs. Draeger all looking at Lam like that? Waiting, on edge, devastated.

Even her mother was staring at her lap, draped in sudden sadness.

And Lam? Her lungs emptied. It was back. The same look she'd seen that night in the kitchen. Almost haunted. What had happened to him? Whatever it was, the pain was there—blinding and horrible—on his face. It took everything she had not to go to him. It wasn't her place—no matter how incredible those kisses had been.

"Syrup, peez, Cowboy-Man?" Jilly looked up at Lam. "See my manners?"

Lam nodded. "They're mighty impressive manners." He winked.

Gwen's heart turned over and, all at once, the room seemed to relax.

Jilly grinned wide. "We make you grumpy?"

Lam chuckled then. "Am I grumpy?"

Jilly and Amy exchanged looks then both shook their heads, curls bouncing.

"Guess it's working then." Lam reached for the French toast, stacking an impressive pile onto his plate.

"Lambert Draeger. You use your best manners, like the girls." Mrs. Draeger clucked her tongue. "I swear, Son, you were not raised in a barn."

"Actually, Mom," Macon interrupted. "We did spend most of our time out there."

Which earned a laugh from everyone.

Gwen sat between Amy and Lam, making sure the girls

had everything they needed before serving herself.

"Gwen, you got just the right amount of bacon in here." Macon pointed at the casserole with his fork.

Her mother shook her head. "She used twice as much as the recipe called for."

"It was only a pound." She couldn't resist glancing Lam's way.

His blue eyes crinkled at the corners as his grin turned dangerous. "A pound, huh?"

She shot him a smile but refused to get all doe-eyed and red-cheeked with an audience.

"Well, I like it." Macon scooped up a massive bite.

"That little pot has that melted chocolate-hazelnut spread you like, Mrs. Draeger." Gwen had placed the pretty little blue-and-white crockery pitcher within easy reach of the woman's seat. Adelaide Draeger didn't just like chocolate—she *loved* chocolate. Gwen was doing her best to incorporate it into meals whenever possible. In moderation, of course.

"Momma made it," Amy said, spearing some French toast with her fork.

"Gwen, you're spoiling me." The woman's smile was warm. "And I appreciate it."

"Good job, Momma," Jilly said between bites.

Amy held up both thumbs again, her mouth too full to talk.

"It is delicious, Gwen. If you do decide to stay, I could retire and be a full-time grandmother." Her mother sounded so excited, Gwen didn't know what to say.

"Jax wants us to stay." Amy was looking at the dog sitting by her chair.

"I think you're right, Amy." Macon studied the dog. "He looks like he's smiling to me. He doesn't smile at everyone."

"Not that we're wanting to get rid of you, Miss Marta. Not at all," Tabby sounded off. "You are family, and we love you. If I do convince Gwen to start catering for me, she won't be able to do all the cooking here, too."

This was too big a decision to make at breakfast, with her girls listening in. Whatever was decided, it would be her decision. "I think Jax is hoping you'll drop some toast." Gwen nodded at the dog. "And he might be interested in going on the fairy hunt you were talking about earlier." It was a pathetic attempt to change the conversation, but she had no choice. She took a sip of her coffee and served herself a piece of French toast.

"If I were going to look for fairies, I'd start in the peach orchard." Tabby smiled at the girls.

"Fairies eat peaches?" Lam looked doubtful.

Gwen almost laughed at the look Tabby shot Lam.

But the girls shrugged. They looked so adorable with their little wire and mesh wings and the outfits Brie had made them. Brie hadn't just been their neighbor, she'd been a real-life knight in shining armor. When Dominic left, she'd taken them in. Not only had she let the girls play with the fabric remnants from her costuming side job, she'd used every scrap of fabric she had to make fantastical princess gowns for the girls.

Brie was doing well. She'd texted a few times. The last time was to say goodbye before she set off on her semester abroad. Gwen made her promise to send postcards—Gwen'd always loved postcards.

Someday she'd travel again, with the girls. It was one of the things she'd promised herself when things got super bleak. An escape really.

"Come see, Cowboy-Man." Jilly smiled. "Pleez. Pleez."

"Cowboy-Man is all work and no play." Macon winked.

Lam leaned back and crossed his arms over his chest. "Someone has to work around here."

"It would do you some good, Lam." Mrs. Draeger seemed to study her son. "You're allowed to have fun now and then."

Gwen was tempted to point out that fairy hunting might not be Lam's idea of fun. He was a grown man, after all, and the girls weren't his. He did deserve to have some fun—but the adult sort of fun. A night out. Then again, he hadn't been at dinner for a while. He might have gone into town. Might have visited friends. Might have a girlfriend.

No. No girlfriend.

She might not know Lam well, but she knew him well enough to know that he wasn't the cheating sort. He was true blue.

"Peez," Amy added.

"Girls." She shook her head. "Cowboy-Man has a lot of work to do. He has a big job that takes a lot of time. I'm sure he wishes he had the time to go with you, but don't make him feel bad if he can't go."

Amy and Jilly put on their brave faces. All that did was make them look pitifully sad and pathetic. Chins quivering. Wide eyes. Slumped little wing-wearing shoulders.

Lam groaned.

Macon and Tabby laughed.

"I'll go." He picked up his fork. "But first, I'm eating all of this French toast."

The girls clapped their hands and went back to eating, the conversation shifting to Macon's work as a fireman and whether or not he had a spotted dog to ride in his fire truck.

She shifted in her chair, her knee knocking Lam's. Out of motherly instinct, she reached under the table to rub his knee—like she'd do for either of the girls. But her hand met his hand and all motherly thoughts vanished. His fingers, work-roughened and warm, threaded with hers and wrapped around her hand. His thumb swept across the back of her hand in slow, gentle strokes. With a final squeeze, he let go and sat back in his chair.

It happened so fast, it was almost like it hadn't happened. He never acknowledged her—didn't even look her way. But she knew it happened. And, even hours later, she could feel the slide of his fingers and the brush of his thumb against her skin.

Chapter Eight

L AM READ THE names again. Veronica and Kendra Hines. Veronica was the mother. Kendra the girl. She was about six or seven, from the looks of it. They were the people his father had been sending money to. And they didn't live in Arizona anymore. They'd moved to Houston. Right here in Texas. Close enough to go see for himself, if he wanted to.

Did he?

Lam studied the two photos, truly torn.

What was he supposed to do? There'd been no note, no special instructions—if he hadn't noticed the regular payments for himself, Lam wouldn't know anything about them. Did they rely on the money? Was he now responsible for their upkeep?

The question was, who were they? What were they to his father?

He scrubbed a hand over his face and sat back in the rocking chair. Jax nudged his hand so Lam gave the dog an obliging rub down. "It's all right," he murmured, wanting to believe it.

He sipped his coffee, turning his attention to the sun breaking over the trees. From the low hum of the cicadas and already warm breeze, it was going to be a scorcher. He needed to check the water level of the tanks. They needed a good, soaking rain—sooner versus later. Might as well check the windmills, too, fix anything that needed fixing.

That was one thing about this place he could count on. When something broke, he could fix it. He could handle it. But this thing with this woman? And the little girl, Kendra? He didn't know what to do about that…them.

"Lost in thought?" Gwen's voice was low, but he still startled. "Sorry," she whispered.

He chuckled, looking up to find her, pot of coffee in hand, leaning out the back door. "Morning."

"I saw the coffee." She held it up as she crossed to his chair. "Ready for a refill?"

"Thank you." Seeing her loosened some of the knots in his stomach and chest.

Jax circled her, tail wagging.

"You a coffee drinker, too?" Gwen asked the dog. "I'm pretty sure it's not good for you. But I might be able to come up with something more dog friendly?"

Jax sat.

"I think that's a please," Lam watched the exchange.

"You think?" Her brows rose.

"It's definitely a please." He chuckled again, nodding his thanks when his mug was full.

Gwen lingered, her gaze falling to his lap. "She's lovely. Pretty little girl."

He tapped the picture against his jean clad thigh. "Yep," he snapped. They were. He'd noticed that. Veronica was pretty and young. Probably Tabby's age. Gwen's age. And, like Gwen, a single mother.

"You okay?" She sat in the chair opposite him, elbows

resting on her knees, like she had all the time in the world.

He nodded, giving himself a minute to study her. Her hair was twisted up, large combs holding it in place, but there were already curls slipping free. She wore a dress—she usually wore a dress. She had great calves. He'd noticed more than once. Today's dress was blue with different size white hearts all over it. It dipped low enough in the front to provide a hint at the curves beneath. But her feet were bare.

"You shoulder a lot around here." It was a statement.

He waited, watching her face. Gwen wasn't one to mask her expressions. With her, he knew exactly where he stood. But she was doing her best to school her features so he was beyond curious to see what was coming.

"No, you do." She shrugged. "That's all. It's impressive."

"Thank you." The compliment threw him. "The place won't run itself."

She nodded. "I get that. Just don't let it consume you."

"Says the woman who's cooking at two in the morning." He took a sip.

She laughed. "If I admit that's something I do for myself, is that weird?"

"Coming from anyone else, probably." He liked hearing her laugh. "But you? No. I've seen you in the kitchen. And I've tasted your cooking."

Her gaze dipped to the picture again. "Can I say something?"

The way she was looking at the pictures? No. But he held his tongue.

"It's none of my business and I probably shouldn't mention it but...you get this look sometimes and—" She broke off, her gaze locking with his. "My heart hurts for you."

Now he couldn't say a word, that damn jagged lump in his throat was back.

"I've been told I'm a really good listener." She swallowed. "And if you ever want to talk, Lam, I'd really like to listen. I... I know life doesn't always turn out the way you thought it will and sometimes the bumps in the road turn into sinkholes that swallow you whole..." She broke off, as if realizing she'd said too much, and tore her gaze from his to stare at her toes. "Don't try to take it on alone if you don't have to."

He heard the regret in her voice. "Is that why you came home? Because you were alone?"

"I've never been so alone." She nodded. "My pride prevented me from asking for help and from coming back here. But pride wouldn't put food in the girls' tummies or give them a safe place to sleep."

He wasn't sure what he'd expected to hear, but this wasn't it. The idea she painted of her and the girls, hungry and alone, turned his stomach. And kicked his anger into high gear. What about the girls' father? Where was that bastard when his daughters were hungry? "Your mom said you had a good job—"

"The best." She glanced his way, then went back to staring at her toes. "I was a sous chef for Dominic Fournier, a brilliant chef. I was enamored. He was, too—briefly, but my weight bothered him, and my pregnancy freaked him out." Another shrug. "My pregnancy was complicated, so I stopped working, and he insisted I stay home with the girls when they were born. They were small, fragile, and they needed me." She broke off for a moment, but Lam waited, knowing there was more. "Dominic made me doubt myself. I gave him that power. I didn't push back, because he was really good at convincing me he was right and I was wrong. According to him, I was wrong a lot." There was an edge to her voice. "When I finally got up the nerve to leave, he took off for a new job in New York, left a note in the mailbox, and an empty bank account. An eviction notice arrived a few days later. Our neighbor let us stay with her for a while, but she was headed off on a semester abroad—Brie, a fashion student. Super talented." She smoothed her skirts with a smile. "I don't know when or why I realized he was the one who had been wrong and that coming home was the right thing, the only thing, that made sense." She shook her head. "Being here, with my mom...I can get strong again. Believe in myself again. Save some money. Figure out where I belong. Let the girls be girls, without all the stress."

Gwen was one of the most confident people he'd ever met, or so he'd thought. But the comments about her weight, believing in herself, and getting strong again told him otherwise. If he ever met Dominic what's-his-name, he'd show him what an old-fashioned butt-kicking was all about. Away from the girls, of course.

"I just dumped all of that on you." She looked horrified.

"I'm glad you told me." He leaned forward to take her hand. "I mean it."

She squeezed his hand, then pulled hers away. "Now you know my story. If you want to share yours, you know where to find me. Any time, Lam." She stood, her brown eyes sweeping over his face before she headed to the back door.

She'd shared something deeply personal with him, and it hadn't been easy. It was a gift, of sorts. How long had it been since he'd felt this comfortable with someone? Too damn long. He didn't want her to go. "This woman." He cleared his throat.

Gwen stopped and turned to face him.

"My father was sending her and the little girl money." He stood, crossing the porch to lean against the rough cedar railing. "I'm trying not to jump to conclusions, but I can only come up with a couple of options, and none of them are good. My father...well, you knew my father. He was a black and white, what's right is right, and wrong is wrong sort of man. And this, she makes him a liar. And our family a joke."

"Not your family. Don't go there." Gwen's brow furrowed "You have to find out, though, don't you? So, you know, I mean really *know*, why he was supporting her?"

He blew out a long, slow breath. "I guess."

"Your mom? Your family?" She came back, setting the coffeepot on her chair, and walking to his side.

He shook his head, aching to hold her now that she was within reach.

"Lam." Her hand rested on his forearm. "You should talk to them. This isn't your burden to bear."

He covered her hand with his. "I know. And I will. But I'd rather come to them with facts rather than questions loaded with all sorts of painful speculation and uncertainty. I need to spare them that. My dad and I didn't see eye to eye on many things, but, for us, family always came first." Bitterness flooded his mouth. "At least, I thought we had that in common."

"Can I do anything?" It was whisper. "Other than oat-meal raisin cookies, you like brownies, right?"

He chuckled. "Yeah."

"I'll get started on those after breakfast." She smiled up at him, so pretty in the morning sun, he was breathless.

His hand lifted, hovering by her cheek.

She stepped closer, sliding her arms around his waist and resting her head against his chest. "I know it doesn't help—"

"No, it does." More than she knew. He closed his eyes and held her close. How could he explain that, in the short time she'd been here, she'd softened what was left of his shattered heart? Good or bad, it was true.

She shuddered against him, her hands pressing against his back.

And there was that. The jolt her touch inspired. The hum of current between them. How she could soothe him and stir his blood at the same time was a mystery, but it was a fact. He turned, brushing his nose along her temple. Another shudder. This time her hands twisted in the fabric of his white undershirt.

"I should start breakfast." Her voice was low and husky and her hold on his shirt didn't ease in the slightest. She was no more ready to let go than he was.

"You should kiss me." He tipped her chin up, searching her face for signs of resistance.

There was none.

"Okay." She nodded. "I'd rather do that."

He was smiling when his lips met hers. Soft and sweet. Warm. She fit, like this, pressed against him. When her hands slid beneath his shirt, a soft moan slid from her mouth into his. That did it. Before he knew it, he'd pulled the combs from her hair and twined the thick curls around one hand, anchoring her there—against him, kissing him, where he could breathe her in.

Her lips were soft.

The side of her jaw, the shell of her ear, and her earlobe were silk. His mouth explored each while his hands cradled her close. He couldn't get enough of her. Her soft moan, the hitch in her breath when he sucked her earlobe into his mouth, or the slight dig of her nails into his back when his tongue traced the curve of her neck. He wanted to soak it all in.

But the sun was rising higher, and the house wouldn't be sleeping for much longer.

He cradled her face between his hands, breathing hard and wishing like hell they had a few hours. Something told him he'd need a hell of a lot more time with her. With her lips parted and her cheeks flushed, she was the picture of temptation. His hunger reflected in her eyes.

"I could keep this up all day." And if she kept looking at him like that, that might be exactly what happened.

"I'm okay with that." She stepped closer, covering his hands with hers. "Really, Lam. I… I feel alive in your arms."

After hearing that, there was only one thing to do. He kissed her. Again. And again.

GWEN WAS SURE of one thing: this was what kissing should be like. All passion and sensation. She wasn't worried about the width of her waist or her kissing ability or...anything. She was holding on to Lam, period.

With each touch, she was further lost in him. The slide of his fingers through her hair. His hand cupping the base of her head. One thickly muscled arm sliding around her waist and drawing her ever closer. He was slow, deliberate—as if he was determined to explore every inch of her. Oh, how she hoped he would.

She slid her hands up his arms, over his shoulders, and down his sides. She'd untucked the skintight white under-shirt he was wearing earlier, so it was all too easy to slip her hands underneath. His warmth singed her fingertips, rolling over her to set her insides ablaze.

His tongue trailed along her lower lip, and her fingers pressed against his back. She wanted more. She wanted...Lam. The thrill of his tongue against hers had her bare toes curling against the wooden porch. He tilted his head, just enough to deepen the kiss and have her swaying into him for support.

Little things like the click-clack of Jax's nails on the wooden porch, the light squeak of the back door, and a disappointed "I smell coffee," didn't seem to matter in Lam's arms.

It was the, "It's out here," followed by a chuckle, that had Lam releasing her so fast, she'd have crumpled to the ground if he hadn't steadied her.

They weren't alone.

Tabby was in shock, her blue eyes wide, as she looked back and forth between the two of them.

Macon was doing his best not to laugh—and failing.

"Don't mind us." Macon held up his hands. "We were looking for the coffee." He pointed at the pot, still resting in the chair where she'd deposited it in her hurry to comfort Lam. "I'll get it and we'll get out of your hair so you can get back to doing whatever it was you were doing."

Oh no. No, no, no. This couldn't happen. She couldn't do this—they couldn't do this. For one thing, he was her boss. And he was dealing with the recent death of his father. And then there was the whole mystery woman. No, getting involved, even physically, was a bad idea. Even if it was the best and most tempting bad idea ever.

"Breakfast." The word came out of nowhere. It took a few seconds before she realized she was the one that said it. "I need to make breakfast." Because she worked here. This was her job. And she'd just been caught kissing her boss.

She was not going to make eye contact with Macon. Or Tabby.

She was definitely not going to make eye contact with Lam.

She was going to make breakfast. Then, possibly, hide in her bedroom until she could decide what to do next. Without another word, she walked into the kitchen, tied the strings of her cupcake-print apron around her neck and waist, and began pulling bowls from cabinets.

Breakfast. She'd had a plan…

Cinnamon rolls with cream cheese icing. Sausage and biscuits with gravy. That was it. Easy.

But her hands wouldn't stop shaking.

Tabby came in minutes later, the forgotten coffeepot in hand. She poured it out, refilled the machine, and started brewing a fresh pot. "I'm really sorry, Gwen—"

Gwen held her hand up. "What you saw"—was amazing—"was wrong." But that didn't stop it from being magical. "And it was a mistake." An incredible, wonderful mistake. "It won't happen again." It couldn't. Once Lam started kissing her, she was a goner. Happily, eagerly, ready and willing to lose herself, and her self-control, in his arms. "I... We..." They what? Were attracted to one another? "It was a mistake." She cracked an egg into the flour and began whisking with vigor.

"Are you sure about that?" Tabby fiddled with the jar of cinnamon.

She blew a curl from her forehead. Where were her combs? Probably on the porch, where he'd dropped them, right before he'd buried his hands in her hair.

"Gwen?" Tabby nudged her.

"Yes?"

"I asked if I could give you a hand." Her blue eyes were studying her.

Considering how scattered she was at the moment? "Yes, please. You can crack ten eggs into that bowl."

Tabby started cracking. "I invited that bride I was telling you about out for tea today. Like a high tea thing, if you're up for it? She's bringing a few of her bridal party and one of them, get this, works for that cable cooking channel."

"She does?" Gwen tried to sound interested, but her body was still aching for Lam, her heart had an odd pang, and her brain wasn't sure what to do about any of it.

"Priscilla, the bride, told me they're considering using the wedding on their wedding special—for the network.

Which would be great for the ranch and my side of the business. And I thought, if you were still considering my suggestion, that you might be interested in whipping up something super-impressive to serve to them?"

Gwen paused, the enormity of Tabby's words sinking in. "I'm cooking for a potential client?" She waited for Tabby's nod. "A potential client who might get my food on television?"

Tabby smiled. "Exactly."

"Are you sure?" She was more than a little stunned. "This could be a big deal for the ranch, Tabby. I don't want my cooking to affect their decision one way or the other."

"Oh, please." Tabby shook her head. "Your cooking will only seal the deal. In fact, I'm counting on it."

"No pressure then." But she was smiling. If there was one thing she was certain of, it was her cooking. "A fancy tea? Finger sandwiches, tiny cakes, chocolate truffles, scones and clotted cream? That sort of thing?"

Tabby nodded. "At four?"

Gwen went back to mixing. "What about a few cake samples? It is for a wedding, after all."

"Like a cake tasting?" Tabby nodded.

"I'm in." Macon came in, pulled out a stool, and sat the counter. "What kind of cake are we tasting?"

"You are not invited." Tabby waved her pointer finger at him. "Today is a big deal, and I don't need you making trouble."

"I'm not the troublemaker." Macon frowned. "Kolton's not here, remember? The coffee ready yet?"

She almost added a second teaspoon of baking soda to

SASHA SUMMERS

the dough when Lam walked inside...in his skintight undershirt. And his tousled dark hair and unshaven jaw.

"Want some?" Tabby asked, refilling both men's mugs.

"Why is today such a big deal?" Macon's question had Tabby detailing all the plans she had for the ranch.

Tabby had always been motivated, even in grade school. She had notebooks full of to-do lists, a record of her wants, and chart of her long-term goals. Gwen wondered what happened to Tabby's notebooks and how many of the things she'd planned she'd managed to check off her to-do list.

The cinnamon rolls were baking. The eggs were cooking. She was not watching Lam run his fingers through his hair. And the skillet for the sausage was almost hot enough.

"Lam, you'd better put on a shirt before Mom gets up." Tabby waved a hand up and down. "And shave. You know how she is."

Lam nodded, shot her a long, lingering look, and left the kitchen.

Apparently, she wasn't the only one that saw the look.

Macon was chuckling behind his coffee cup, and Tabby was shaking her head.

She mumbled a lame excuse and headed into the large pantry. Since she didn't really need anything, she waited a few seconds, grabbed some nonstick spray but hesitated by the door when she heard Tabby say, "Stop it, Macon. Don't mess this up for him."

She wanted to argue, she did. But Tabby's next words made her pause a moment longer.

"After all the heartache and loss he's suffered, he deserves some happiness." Tabby's voice was stern, but loving. "There

120

are days I worry his heart will never heal."

"You think this is a good idea?" Macon asked. "What is he falls for her and she leaves? Then he gets kicked to hell again. I don't want to see him like that, Tabs. He was a ghost for so long."

She was eavesdropping now, plain and simple, and it was wrong. Whatever had happened to Lam, this wasn't how she wanted to find out about it. Learning he'd had his heart broken explained a few things but, deep down, she suspected there was more to it.

By the time the cinnamon rolls were golden, the girls arrived with her mother. Their sweet chatter filled the room and brought smiles all around. She hurried to her room long enough to pull on her well-worn Mary Janes, and returned to the kitchen to find the table set and the eggs and sausage in serving dishes.

Lam was helping the girls stack up the cinnamon rolls on a platter, his hair combed, jaw shaved, and buttoned up in a starched shirt. The sight of the three of them, smiling and laughing, made that pang in her heart a little sharper.

Yesterday, he'd spent an hour with them in the peach orchard looking for fairies before a phone call pulled him away. At dinner, he'd asked if they'd had any luck finding fairies and tried to bolster their spirits by telling them about a new calf that had been born. As a result, all through bath and bedtime, the girls had chattered on about meeting the baby cow—and naming it.

She gave her girls a smile. "Thank you." Her gaze met Lam's.

"You're welcome." His voice was low and deep and

husky and delicious. And the way he looked at her, especially her mouth, made her wobble on her low heels. "Thank you for the cinnamon rolls. They smell good."

"Cuz Momma made 'em," Jilly said.

"Bestest cook," Amy added.

"If I am, it's because I learned it from your gramma," she told the girls.

"Does Gramma make cinnamon rolls an' choc-o-lot chips?" Amy asked.

"Chocolate chips?" Lam asked.

"Only a few. For your mom." It was impossible not to smile at him.

He shook his head. "Your mom is pretty special, you know that?" He was talking to the girls, but looking at her.

"Cuz she cooks good?" Jilly asked. "Taking us fairy hunting? Soon."

"Yup, fairies." Amy grinned. "And tells us stories?"

"That's part of it." His blue gaze was unwavering.

"What's the holdup with the cinnamon rolls?" Macon called from the table. "Mom's over here with her stomach growling."

"Macon, stop." Mrs. Draeger giggled. "Though those cinnamon rolls smell divine."

The girls carried the platter to the table together, taking teeny-tiny steps and great care with their delivery. Gwen watched, loving how at ease they'd become with this kind and generous family.

"Need help?" Lam asked, his fingers working the knots of her apron free, and brushing along her neck and ear, waist and hip. "You smell like cinnamon." The whisper set her nerves afire.

"Hungry, Cowboy-Man?" Jilly's voice rang out, loud and cheerful. "Cinnamonomon roll for you?"

"Yes, please," he answered.

Gwen followed, her senses reeling, to take her seat between him and Jilly.

"Oh, Gwen, this smells so good," Tabby said.

"Good enough to eat." Lam took a cinnamon roll and bit into it with gusto, smiling a downright wicked smile her way.

Chapter Nine

RASCAL HAD BEEN a pain in Lam's rear since the day he'd arrived on the ranch. Being over seventeen hundred pounds of bull made him a formidable adversary. His horns made him downright dangerous. When that bull got mad, keeping a wide berth was the best course of action for all. But the fool had tried to go over a fence—considering his size, it was hard to imagine that—and landed himself in a pasture with a bevy of beautiful cows for him to...court.

Lam got the news from Old John, one of ranch hands, as they were clearing the breakfast table. Old John was as weathered as they came—he'd been old and weathered since Lam could remember. He didn't say much, and was crusty, but downright magic when it came to cattle. If John couldn't get Rascal out of the pasture, it wasn't going to be pretty. When Lam heard Old John had called in their two most reliable cattlemen, Hugo and Clint, he knew this was an all-hands-on-deck situation. Old John wasn't the sort to ask for help, period.

"Bad bull?" Amy asked.

Old John nodded. "Rascal's a son-of-a—"

"Meanie," Tabby cut him off.

Old John didn't approve of her edited insult, the scowl on his deeply lined face was hard to miss. But he let it go.

Which was good, because, when he did talk, Old John cussed like a sailor.

"Go ahead and get the trailer hooked up on the truck." Lam sighed. "Hugo can drive. Get Clint to saddle Earl."

"I'll come." Macon was up.

Lam saw the circles under Macon's eyes. "We've got this. You just came off duty at the fire station. You catch up on some sleep. Don't want Rascal to tenderize you."

It was Macon's turn to scowl. "Really?"

"Fine." Lam shook his head. "Let's go." From the corner of his eye, he saw Amy and Jilly, all wide-eyed and anxious. "Don't fret, girls, Old John normally scares Rascal enough to get him running into the trailer."

Old John turned on his booted heel and pushed through the back door, muttering under his breath.

"Now, you've done it." But Macon was smiling. "Get him in a bad mood and he's meaner than a snake."

"How could you tell?" Gwen asked. "That he's in a bad mood, I mean?" She tucked a curl, still loose down her back, behind her ear. An ear he'd enjoyed nibbling on not too long ago.

"I'm pretty sure Old John is always in a bad mood." Tabby was carrying plates to the kitchen counter.

"True." Lam nodded. "It's all about varying degrees. Surly to meaner than a snake." He shrugged. "Guess we'll see."

"Well, be careful." His mother piped up. "That bull makes me nervous. Too many close calls in the past."

Lam hoped she'd stop there. There was no point worrying the girls. Rascal was all snort and charge, but, so far, no rider or horse had ever seen the sharp end of one of his horns. "Yes, ma'am. Thanks for breakfast, Gwen."

Her cheeks turned a charming pink. Damned if she wasn't always charming to him.

He and Macon were riding out to the north pasture five minutes later. The triple-digit heat made the horizon ripple, and there were no clouds in the bright blue sky for cover. But the beauty of his home never failed to amaze him.

Clumps of cedar sprung up now and then, no matter how many times they'd chop them down. Between the limestone outcrops and cactus, there was no calling their place gentle—but it was beautiful all the same. The land stretched in all directions. Rolling hills, oak and pecan and peach trees, and a sprinkling of windmills, fences, and cows, as far as the eye could see.

"So." Macon pushed his hat back. "Gwen."

He shook his head. He'd been surprised when his brother hadn't teased him this morning. He'd had plenty of time after Tabby and Gwen had left them alone. Instead, they'd stood in companionable silence while he pulled himself together.

Not that he'd pulled himself together. She'd gotten to him. Gwen. And, dammit all, he didn't mind.

"Go ahead and shake your head." Macon chuckled. "I saw it. I saw you. You're sweet on her."

Lam didn't argue. There was no point. Besides, Macon was right.

"I just wanna make sure this isn't about her girls."

He could hear the struggle in his brother's voice. They all danced around the subject of Grant's death, for his sake he supposed, but they'd all lost him—all loved him. Instead of getting testy over his brother's question, he took it for what it was. "You worried about me, little brother?"

Macon nodded. "Guess so."

Lam smiled. "Let me assure you, the last thing I was thinking about this morning was her girls." Gwen had blocked out the rest of the world.

"I got that. And she is gorgeous. Kinda hard not to notice. I'm fine with it. You two get together, she stays, her cooking stays." He shrugged. "I'd say that's a win all around."

She hadn't been there long enough for him to be thinking this way. It had been, what, a week? One week since he'd walked into his kitchen and she'd flipped his world. So why did his brother's suggestion sound right to him? Why did having her in his home make it complete?

"I want you to be happy, Lam. We all do."

Until she and the girls showed up, happiness hadn't been on his radar. When Grant died, that part of him died, too. He took full blame for his marriage falling apart. He couldn't look at Tracy without seeing all they had and lost. And she couldn't stay on the ranch—she'd said there were too many reminders. He hadn't put up much of a fight.

From what he'd heard, she was doing well—married and settled down in Wichita Falls. She'd moved on. Maybe he should too. With Gwen?

The sight of Rascal, peacefully grazing, in the middle of two dozen cows, demanded his full attention. The Brangus was a beast.

It took an hour to get him loaded onto the truck. By that point, he and Earl were covered in sweat. Macon was red faced and wound up. Old John was randomly hurling insults while Hugo stayed behind the wheel of the truck, laughing and shaking his head. The man had an odd sense of humor.

Once Rascal was deposited away from potential lady friends, he and Macon went to work repairing the fence the damn bull hadn't quite cleared. Old John and Hugo knew the drill. The four of them pulled up the old concrete, mixed new, smoothed down stays, and twisted the new barbed wire into place before pulling it tight.

"Ever wish you had a desk job, Old John?" Macon asked.

Old John ignored him.

"With his personality?" Hugo asked. "He'd get fired on the first day."

Lam chuckled, hanging his hat on the fence post and wiping his face with the bandana he kept in his pocket. "Old John is right where he belongs." He nodded at the older man, wondering for the hundredth time just how old the man was. He'd been here since Lam could remember. Hell, the place wouldn't be the same without him.

Old John nodded back.

They worked the rest of the morning then headed to the barn for lunch. Old John and Hugo were self-sufficient men. His mother had given up trying to convince them to join them for meals at the main house years ago. If either of them did wander in for a meal, an extra place was instantly set. But, for the most part, they kept to themselves.

Lunch was canned chili, store-bought corn bread, and gallons of iced tea. Made by Old John, to be eaten-at-your-own-risk.

"Sweet thing in the kitchen," Old John said, surprising

them all. "Who's she for?"

Hugo paused, midchew. "One o' you get hitched?"

Who was she, Gwen, for? His heart answered with absolute certainty. Firmly. No room for doubt. It wasn't a thunderbolt realization or a jarring surprise. It was more an instant acceptance of a truth—an irrefutable, concrete fact.

He was a damn fool.

But how she felt? He'd no idea. Sure, she wanted his kisses, felt alive in his arms, but that didn't mean she cared for him. Wanting and loving were two different things.

"If a Draeger ever gets married, you'd both be there. No arguing." Macon nodded his way. "Her name is Gwen. She's Marta's daughter. And she's his."

Lam almost choked. What the hell was Macon doing?

"Marta's a fine woman." Hugo nodded.

"Mighty fine," Old John agreed, going rigid and glaring at Hugo. "She's not leaving? Marta, I mean?"

Lam wondered at the exchange between the two older men. "No. She's playing grandmother for now. They're still working out if Gwen is staying on as cook or not."

"Good." Hugo nodded. "Grandmother." He smiled.

Old John grunted, relaxing back into his chair.

Hugo and Old John were interested in Marta? Did she know? Had either of them ever spent time with Marta? Lam had no idea.

"And Gwen's not mine." He scooped up another spoonful of chili.

Macon laughed.

Old John shook his head. "Stubborn. Liked the looks of her." He moved his hands in an hour glass shape and winked.

"Time's a wasting boy." Hugo bit into his corn bread.

Lam ignored the exchange, rinsed his dishes, and gave his brother a hard look. "I'm checking the vaccination shed before I head back."

Macon waved, still smiling.

Days like this, when things were weighing on his mind, he enjoyed riding the property. He and Earl rode fence lines, checking the integrity of the wire and looking for issues, while working through the Veronica and Kendra situation. Maybe Gwen was right—maybe he should tell his siblings? But not his mother. He couldn't do it. If there was ever an example of unwavering love, it was that of his mother for his father. Joseph Draeger would have been a difficult man to love, but she had—still did, deeply.

Which made his thoughts turn to Gwen.

He was still puzzling over her relationship with the girls' father. What sort of man would leave his children? He couldn't imagine it. From the day Grant was born, he'd never willingly left his son's side. This Dominic's actions were unconscionable.

Hopefully the girls were too little for their father's desertion to leave too big a wound.

But for Gwen? Damage had definitely been done.

In time, maybe, there'd be a chance for them. If she stayed. If she decided to risk her heart on him. Because the idea of letting Gwen in was beginning to sound all too appealing.

"HOLY CRAP, THIS is sinfully good." Tina Montes was devouring the cake samples Gwen had brought out. "You made these? All of these?"

"Today," Tabby added, beaming.

"This is incredible, Gwen." Priscilla was the bride. A very not-bridezilla bride. She was soft-spoken and calm. "Honestly, I can't thank you enough for doing all of this on such short notice."

"It was my pleasure." Gwen smiled around the table. Eight women, all dressed to the nines, smiled back. There were too many eyes for her liking. In the kitchen, she was in control—trusting her instincts and not worrying about the approval of others. Out here, she felt awkward. With her retro updo and thrift shop dress and, since all them had to be a size four or less, her shape. "I'll leave you to it, then. If you need anything, let me know."

"I already know." Priscilla stood. "I'd really like you to cater my wedding. If it's not too presumptuous, I have a menu I was hoping to serve. If, maybe, you could get us a quote in the next day or two, that would be wonderful. For planning." She handed her a neatly paper-clipped stack of paper. "The budget's in there, too," she whispered.

That was fast. Too fast. Was this what she wanted?

Then again, what did she have to lose?

Gwen smiled and took the packet. "Not presumptuous at all. Efficient. I admire a woman who knows what she wants." With that, she left the formal dining room and returned to the safety of her kitchen.

Her kitchen?

She stared around the room, loving the white-washed

cabinets, high ceilings, marble countertops and stainless appliances. If she'd been asked to design the space, she wouldn't change a thing. Double ovens, convection ovens, warming drawers. And the pantry. It was a room in itself.

Could she see herself here as the family cook? No. Not long term.

Could she see herself here catering fancy events? It wasn't an immediate no. It was more of a maybe.

She unclipped the packet and stared at the number on the paper. This was her *food* budget? For food? Just food? The number was staggering. Mind-blowing. A couple of weddings like this, and she and the girls could start traveling and still let her set some aside for savings.

She wandered to the back of the kitchen, to her mother's reading nook. The girls were napping, so she hoped her mother was here.

"What's up?" Her mother looked up from her book, peering over the edge of her reading glasses.

She handed her mother the paper and sat in the other comfy calico-covered armchair that sat on either side of a small table. The laundry room was adjacent and Gwen was too antsy to sit still, so she hopped back up and busied herself folding and hanging clothes while her mother flipped through the pages.

"Gwen, this is…amazing." Her mother was just as stunned. "Ridiculous to spend that sort of money on a wedding, but amazing for *you*." She crossed her hands in her lap. "What are you going to do?"

Gwen hung a red plaid button-up shirt on a hanger. It was Lam's. It smelled like him. And dryer sheets. She smoothed the front gently, wishing he was here. "I'm not going to say no. How can I? The wedding is next week."

"I'll help you, of course. This is going to be a lot of work." She held up the papers. "Does this mean you're staying? Or is this a one-shot sort of deal?"

She hugged herself, paced the length of the kitchen, and stared out the window. "I don't know, Mom."

Her mother nodded, doing her best not to look disappointed. "Before I forget, you have some mail."

Gwen took the letters, distracted. "I think...can I go for a walk?" she asked. "The lasagna is baking and the bread is rising—"

"Go on, Gwen." Her mother nodded. "Of course, you can take a walk."

"Thanks, Mom." She stooped, kissed her mother's forehead, and headed out the back door into the blazing heat of the Texas sun.

She and the girls had made the trek to the peach orchard a half a dozen times, so she headed the opposite way, following the winding path higher and higher until she came around a corner and wound up on a lookout deck. Several large Adirondack chairs and a massive fire pit sat on the deck, perfect for bonfires and stargazing. The view, up high like this, was breathtaking. She could only imagine how lovely the night sky would be.

It was ruggedly beautiful country. And it was the only place that ever felt like home.

Here, she had everything she'd ever need.

She looked at the letters then...and felt the blood drain from her face. Dominic? How did he know? She tore open the envelope and read the short note. A phone number and two sentences. *We have things to talk about. Call me or I'm coming to Texas.*

Dominic? Here? Why? It was possible he missed the girls...

"They'd be better off with me." His words had chilled her to the bone.

Dominic had taken her dreams and twisted them until they were so knotted, she wasn't sure what was her idea versus his opinion of her idea. He'd been so charming, so dazzling, with his accent and his confidence. In the beginning, teasing had been a form of affection. From her small-town Texas upbringing to her astounding virginal status, he'd seemed enthralled by her. From the beginning he'd been amused by her lack of skill to assuring her he'd help her lose the extra weight, she'd been his 'pet project.' Then he'd gone from being enthralled by her to being obsessed with changing her. Improving her and, when that wasn't enough, controlling her. Taking her phone, then the car, then the credit cards. He seemed to be locking her away, with the girls, so she had no choice but to do what he said. Once she'd come to terms with her reality—that what he was doing wasn't okay—she knew that leaving was the only choice.

No matter how much he'd made her doubt herself, her value and worth, she'd found the strength to do what it took for her girls. She'd never, ever, let them down.

And if he had suddenly decided he wanted to be a father, she would fight to keep them right where they were. With her. With their family.

"I won't let them down." She spoke loudly, firmly.

He was the problem. She and the girls had done nothing wrong. It wasn't their fault that his idea of love meant control. He didn't want them, but he'd wanted to make sure no one else could have them, either. And she'd been too naïve and enamored to see that—then. But that was then. And now... Well, it was up to her now. To let go of the doubts he'd instilled and stop worrying about being perfect, from her weight to her cooking.

It was time to love herself and find out what would make *her* happy.

"Gwen?" Lam said.

He startled her, the letter slipping from her fingers to catch on the breeze.

"Got it." He snagged it with ease, holding it out for her.

Of course, he was here now. He made her happy. But she wasn't sure what that meant in the long run. It seemed too early to start thinking about a future with him. Wasn't it? And now, Dominic's letter... She took the letter, shoving it in her pocket, and inspecting him. "You are a dirty mess."

He was. His straw hat was set low on his forehead, shading his face. The blue plaid button-up shirt he wore was damp. Dirt, dust, and possibly grease streaked his jeans. His boots were covered in a fine limestone dust. He was, every bit, a man. A gorgeous, big, dirty, manly-man.

"Working." He took off his hat and wiped his forehead with the back of his arm. "You okay? You look...upset."

She nodded. Dominic was her problem, not his. But he noticed. He saw. And it felt good.

He didn't look convinced. "Saw you coming up here."

"You did?" She was smiling. "And you decided to follow me?"

He cocked his head, an odd look on his face. "Yeah. I guess I did." He shook his head, grinning.

Oh, that grin and the things it did to her. "Did you want something?"

His brow rose high. "That's an interesting question." He took a step closer.

Her heart was thumping hard now, the spark in his eyes already melting her insides. "I know what you're thinking..." Her voice was husky.

"I bet you do." He was inches away. "Guess that means I don't have to ask?"

She shook her head, closing the distance between them to twine her arms around his neck. "Nope."

He bent his head, his lips featherlight on hers. "I need a shower." He was apologizing—even as he was kissing her.

"A shower? You're rushing things for us, aren't you?" She threaded her fingers through the hair at his nape, watching his eyes widen at her words.

His jaw tightened. "I wasn't...I didn't... Damn." His lips sealed against hers, no longer hesitant. At his soft moan, she parted her lips and hung on. The sweep of his tongue and the tightening of his grip on her lower back had her arching into him.

She liked this Lam, loved the hunger in his kiss and the sureness of his touch, and ached for what came next.

Apparently, it was being swept off her feet. Lam didn't have a problem with it. In his arms, with his mouth pressed to hers, being weightless was a state of mind and body. He sank into the chair, pulled her tight against him, and went back to kissing her.

Gwen nuzzled his neck, the taste of salt and Lam intoxicating. She turned, tugging at her skirts until her leg was free and she could face him—straddling him. Her fingers ran over his shirt front, popping the snaps of his shirt with glee. Until she encountered his undershirt. She deflated a little, tugging at the fabric as her gaze met his.

He was breathing hard, the tick of his jaw muscle giving her chills. But it was the raw need in his blue eyes that had her throbbing.

"You're not rushing things?" he all but growled, glancing at her hands—twisting his undershirt—before devouring her face with his eyes.

Yes, she was. But she didn't care. She shook her head.

The corner of his mouth kicked up, and he leaned forward, letting her push his shirt from his shoulders and tug his undershirt over his head.

She sat back, marveling at the broad expanse of angular muscles and smooth skin. As a man, she was pretty sure she'd never seen or imagined anything like him. How could she? She'd never thought this was real? She pressed her hand against his chest, her fingers trailing across his shoulder before dipping to the place over his heart.

He sat forward to press his lips against hers, noses brushing. She smiled and leaned into his kiss, her hands sliding over his bare skin.

The brush of his fingers on her thighs was a shock to the system. His hands, sliding to her hips, had her shuddering against him.

His tongue delved into her mouth as his hands gripped her hips and pressed her against him. His jeans didn't do a thing to hide how much he wanted her. She arched against him, the friction pulling a moan from them both.

"Gwen," he growled against her neck, his hands holding her in place. "I know we're rushing things now."

She nodded, cradling his head against her chest. He was right. As good as this was, she didn't want either one of them to do something they might later regret. "Guess I got a little carried away."

"I'm okay with that." He pressed another kiss to her throat.

Her laugh was husky. Slowly she straightened, lifting one leg and attempting to stand. But he pulled her back into his lap, holding her against him.

"This is better," he murmured.

"It is?" She was still resting against his glorious naked chest.

"Safer." He chuckled.

She could argue with that. And, truth be told, she was content to be held by him. More than content. Happy. With a sigh, she rested her hand over his heart. It thundered beneath her touch. Exactly like hers.

"Good day?" he asked.

"Did you wrangle Rascal without incident?" She looked up at him. "You need to let your mother know you're okay. She was worrying."

"Now?" he asked.

She nibbled on her lower lip. "If I say no, I'm selfish. If I say yes..." She broke off, horrified at how much she'd revealed to him.

"I need to put my shirt on." He smiled.

"True." But with or without his shirt on, it didn't matter. She wanted to stay this way, to hold on to this for as long as she could.

"He's safe. The cows no longer have to fend for their honor."

That made her laugh.

He kissed her temple. "And I fixed a few fences."

"No wonder you're all sweaty and dirty." She burrowed against his chest.

"It bothers you, I can tell." He chuckled, his arms tightening. "That meeting with Tabby go okay?"

She nodded. "More than okay. They want me to cater the wedding." She looked up at him again. "You should have seen the budget they have, Lam. It's crazy. Like, crazy-crazy."

"That crazy?" He stared down at her, his fingers toying with one of her long, red curls.

"Yes." She tried not to read into that look, tried not to see what she wanted to see on his handsome face. "I've never been married so I don't know the going rate, but this seemed a little exorbitant."

"My wedding was small, her family and mine—no frills." He shrugged. "Seems like most folks getting married here are putting on a show."

"You were married?" Not a surprise, really. He was totally marrying material. But she pegged him as a married-for-life kind of guy.

"Yep." He nodded, his brow furrowing. "A few years back."

"Oh."

"Your mom, my mom, didn't mention…anything?" He cleared his throat.

She felt the slight shift in his posture, stiffening, pulling away. "No. I didn't ask, honestly. I guess, I don't know, it feels like an invasion of privacy—to go poking around in someone's past." Clearly, they were entering dangerous territory.

He nodded, his gaze searching hers. "You going to do it?" He paused. "Cater the crazy, fancy wedding?"

He didn't want to talk about it, whatever *it* was. Message received.

She nodded.

"You made any other decisions?" He paused. "About staying here?"

She drew in a deep breath. If he wasn't ready to talk about his past, surely he'd understand her reluctance to make such a big decision so quickly. *Because making out with him is a far less rash thing to do than committing to a job, right?* She sighed, choosing the easy way out—teasing. "Are you offering me a job?"

He nodded. "You're the only one on the fence about it." He was serious, intent, completely thwarting her teasing thing.

"Lam." She pushed out of his lap to stand. "It's not just me, you know?"

"I do." He stood. "Seems to me your girls are right where they need to be. Hunting fairies. With Jax. With family. People who care. And their momma strong and confident." He paused. "And beautiful."

He thought she was beautiful?

"It's your choice, obviously." He tugged on his under-shirt and picked up the button-up shirt she'd tossed aside. He looked at her, then stared out over the hills and valley below. "I'd like it if you stayed. I'll go check in with my mom." The words were so strung together it took her a minute to realize what he'd said. By then, he was halfway down the path.

Chapter Ten

WEDDING FEVER HIT the ranch. Lam and Macon did their best to stay out of the way but, with the film crew on the property, it wasn't possible. He wasn't sure why anyone would want to watch a television show about someone else's wedding, but it looked like a pretty big deal. And the woman in charge, Tina, knew exactly what she wanted, and had no problem letting them all know about it.

"It's standard," she explained, hands on hips, staring out over the ranch. "Set up the place and get a feel for the setting. You know?"

No, he didn't know.

That didn't stop the woman, her camera, and lighting people from filling his kitchen. Gwen looked every bit as frazzled as he felt. With her hair twisted up high and a bright turquoise dress hugging her every curve, Lam was hard-pressed not to shoo them all out so he could give her a few more reasons to stay right here, with him.

"Has anyone ever told you that you have a unique look?" Tina asked Gwen, walking around her. "The whole pinup girl thing? Sassy. And, honestly, a bit wow-gorgeous."

A *bit*? The woman needed glasses.

"Unique, yes." Gwen frowned. "The rest? No." Her laugh was forced.

"Ever thought about doing television?"

Gwen was laughing then.

"I'm serious." Tina shook her head. "You, looking like you."

Lam wasn't sure what that meant, but he was pretty sure he didn't like it. Anything that took Gwen away from here, he wasn't a fan of. They hadn't had one second alone since that day on the lookout deck and it was taking a toll.

"What are you making?" Tina asked.

Gwen glanced at the camera and swallowed. "Actually, I'm just making dinner. Chicken fried steak."

"My favorite." He nodded. "Good choice."

Up until now, she hadn't seen him. But now she had. And she was smiling at him like a fool. "Think you'll be able to choke it down?"

"Good Texas cooking?" Tina nodded. "Go for it."

"First, the girls and I were going to pick vegetables. From the garden." She glanced Lam's way.

"Garden?" Tina asked. "What girls?"

"This way." Lam led them back out the door and around the house to the kitchen garden. Amy and Jilly were wearing their own little aprons, kneeling beside a large basket, with Marta nearby.

"This is gold." Tina clapped her hands and started issuing orders to the cameraman.

"What is happening?" Gwen whispered to him.

"Guess they're going to make you famous." He stared down at her. "You look pretty in that color."

She blinked.

"Momma." Jilly waved a carrot at her. "Lookie."

"Oh, that one looks perfect." She shot him another mystified look and joined the girls in the garden.

"Mr. Draeger, can you stand out of the shot, please?" Tina waved him to her side.

He went, watching Amy rub every speck of dirt from the vegetables they picked, Jilly collecting just as many bugs as she did vegetables, and Gwen patiently explaining which were ready for picking and which weren't. When Jilly held out a caterpillar and Amy fell backward, he wasn't the only one who laughed.

"A gold mine," Tina said, jotting notes on her phone.

Lam spent the rest of the day in the background. When they headed back into the kitchen, the cameras were rolling, and Gwen started cooking. He could tell she was nervous. Maybe it was having people in her kitchen? Or maybe she was camera shy? Whatever it was, he waited until she looked his way, then winked and gave her a thumbs-up.

Her saucy grin was answer enough.

She did a good job, answering the questions Tina had about what she was cooking while making what promised to be a delicious dinner. Even when his family slipped in and some of the bridal party there for prior wedding footage, Gwen managed to keep it together—looking his way every now and again.

"You're blind," Macon said, nudging him.

"Meaning? Wait, do I want to know?"

"She's looking for you, Lam." He shook his head. "When she gets nervous, she looks for you."

How he wished that were true. If it was, he had reason to hope.

"I think we're good here." Tina was all smiles. "We'll clear out of your kitchen now." She held her hand out to him. "Thank you for your time, Mr. Draeger."

He nodded, worn out from the woman's intensity level. As nice as the payout would be, he was more than ready for this wedding to be over.

Within ten minutes, they were gone and the kitchen returned to normal.

Gwen leaned forward, resting her elbows on the counter and covering her face with her hands. "That was horrible," she said between her hands.

She had no idea how adorable she was.

"Okay, Momma?" Amy asked.

"She's tired, Pumpkin," Marta explained. "Let's get these plates on the table."

"I help." Jilly went running to Marta's side.

"You were a natural," Tabby argued. "Priscilla said Tina is all fired up about you. She can't wait for everyone to taste your food. It's going to be amazing, Gwen. You'll see."

Gwen peeked through her fingers. "Okay." Her gaze met his and she straightened, smiling and shrugging.

"You did real good." Which was an understatement. She'd been enchanting. He wasn't much of a television watcher, but he'd sure as hell tune in to see how sweetly she smiled at her girls, how knowledgeable she was about cooking, and for one of those saucy grins he loved.

"Thank you." She was nibbling on her lower lip, her gaze falling to the snaps on his shirt.

He ran a hand over his snap buttons and bit back a curse. He knew what she was thinking. And, now, dammit, so was he.

"Still no fairy," Tabby was saying as he took his seat at the table. "I've put out hummingbird nectar, like you said, Marta, but nothing yet. We'll keep looking, girls. There's bound to be a fairy sooner or later."

"Maybe it's too hot for them?" Mrs. Draeger asked. "You know, delicate things tend to stay out of the sunlight and heat."

"We find 'em," Jilly agreed.

Amy perked up.

"They're probably just hiding," Macon added. "Too many people with the wedding."

Lam agreed wholeheartedly. "He's got a point, Amy."

"Stick in the mud," Tabby teased. "You've never been much for crowds. Even when you were riding, you were quick to hightail it out of there when there were too many people around."

"That was a long time ago." Another lifetime.

"Did you know Cowboy-Man used to ride bulls?" Macon asked the girls.

"Not supposed to." Jilly shook her head.

"Horses. Not bulls." Amy looked confused. And precious.

"That's right," he agreed. "Don't ever ride a bull. Bad idea." He shot Tabby a look. The last thing he needed to worry about was the girls trying to ride a bull.

"Right." Tabby nodded. "Right. Cowboy-Man has a nasty ol' scar on his leg from a big, mean bull."

He felt Gwen's hand on his knee. A thank-you squeeze, nothing more. But he caught her hand in his and held on.

The sliding of fingers and stroke of her thumb along his wrist had him struggling for control.

The fact that she was staring at his snap buttons again, wasn't helping.

Dinner seemed to drag on forever. Not because of the company or the conversation, but because his body had an agenda all its own. The sooner he could get in a long, cold shower, the better.

Gwen wasn't helping. When he brought dishes into the kitchen, she'd been loading the dishwasher, bent forward— all curves and invitation. Every time she smiled his way, he took one more step toward his breaking limit.

"Clean," Jilly said.

"Good dinner." With a nod, he left the kitchen and headed to his room and his shower, where he stood under the spray for a good fifteen minutes.

GWEN WAS TERRIFIED. And excited.

She'd never, ever set out to seduce someone. But tonight, after she'd tucked the girls in, she'd shaved, styled her hair, flossed and brushed her teeth, and put on makeup, then stared at herself in the mirror wondering what she was doing. But she knew. She ached for Lam, something she'd never experienced before.

Because he saw her, wanted her, as she was.

Was it really a seduction when it was plain he wanted this as much as she did? She wasn't sure, but she was about to find out. Armed with a plate of freshly baked oatmeal raisin cookies and wearing her rainbow pajama top, she crept the halls of the ranch house to Lam's office. That was the worst part.

What if Mrs. Draeger came out?

Or Macon? They'd never hear the end of it then.

But she made it to the office undiscovered. Light spilled out from under the door. Good, he was still awake.

Her nerves almost had her rethinking this. Almost.

But today had been different, for her anyway. All today, she'd sought him out. Seeing him there, calm and supportive, had made her believe she could do anything. And she had.

With painfully slow movements, she turned the knob and opened the office door.

Lam lay sprawled on his couch, an arm thrown across his face, snoring softly. His boots sat on the floor. Paperwork was spread out across the coffee table and more was stacked on the floor. As disappointed as she was, she understood.

Tabby had shared a little of the steps he was taking to up the Draegers' stakes in the rodeo stock game. Not just steer and bronc horses, but bulls. Lam was determined to make a go of it, something his father had resisted.

She set the plate on the Lam's desk, shushed Jax with the dog chew she'd brought for him, and read over the large whiteboard on the far wall—names and dates and stud fees and bloodlines. It was a web of lines and notes that made her eyes cross. This was big business. Serious money and serious respect.

Lam was all about respect.

Which made her sneaking, wearing a so not-sexy tent-sized pajama top, into his office to seduce him more than a little ironic.

Jax whimpered, so she crouched, giving the dog a deep rubdown. The dog stared at her with golden eyes.

"You're judging me?" she whispered.

"He's been known to do that." Lam's voice was thick with sleep. His arm rested above his head now, but he hadn't moved.

She winced. "I wasn't going to wake you."

His brows rose, traveling slowly from her toes to her face.

"I was hoping you were awake," she confessed.

"Believe me, I'm awake now." He stood, crossing to her, reaching around her for a cookie. "Still warm?"

She smiled.

He bit into it, moaning softly. "You play dirty, Gwen Hobbs. You're after something."

"On the contrary, Cowboy-Man. I'm being very straightforward about this." She swallowed. "I'm prepared to use whatever means necessary to get you to take me to bed—"

The cookie hit the floor and she was tugged against his chest.

No holding back. Not now. His hand twined in her hair, and she slid her hands between them, gripping his shirt front and pulling. The snaps popped free, and her fingers brushed skin. Skin?

She pulled back. "No undershirt?"

"You weren't the only one with plans tonight." He pushed the collar of her pajama top aside and pressed a kiss to her shoulder. It was long and lingering, with the brush of his tongue. "I figured I'd need a power nap first."

She laughed, a soft, breathless laugh. But she held her breath as his hand skimmed along the front of her pajama top to rest beneath her breast.

He kissed the spot beneath her ear. "You wanted a bed—"

"Or a desk. A couch." His mouth latched onto her earlobe. "The...floor." As long as he didn't stop.

"No." His hands moved up, barely grazing the tips of her breasts, before cradling her face. "My bed."

She clung to his hand as he led her down the hall a few steps and into his room. He closed and locked the door, giving her a second to inspect Lam's room. A lamp in the corner was on, casting a low glow over the interior. Very manly. Leather and dark wood, spacious and minimalist. A few framed photos on his dresser. A clock. Not much else. Everything seemed oversized—because Lam was a big man. But the only thing that mattered was the massive bed on the far wall. The bed he was leading her toward.

But the closer they got, the louder her insecurities became. Dominic had planted so many doubts and fears in her head about her body and her sexuality. And, right now, they were playing through her mind.

"Gwen?"

"Yes." That horrible, high-pitched squeak was back.

The bedside lamp clicked on.

"What's wrong?" he asked, cradling her cheek.

She shook her head.

"Tell me, please." The tenderness in his voice was what did it. "Gwen?"

"I...I've only ever slept with him." She cleared her throat. "And he had a lot of opinions about this. Me. My body. My…skill. Now…You and me. And I'm worried I'll be…a disappointment."

He stared at her, his jaw so rigid, she was afraid for his teeth. His hands slid through her hair. "You could never disappoint me. You're beautiful. All of you." He swallowed. "I don't know what to do here. Show you how bad I want you or hold on to you until we're asleep or you're feeling the urge to seduce me again."

She smiled a little. He meant it. Because Lam was a good and decent man. A hot, good and decent man, whose kisses set her on fire. "I know it's different with you. You look at me—really see me—and want me. As I am."

He nodded. "I'll wait until you're sure this is what you want."

Wait! That's what started all of this. She didn't want to wait anymore. She wanted this, maybe even *needed* it. Now. "This is what I want. You are what I want." She swallowed, pushing the collar of her top aside and wriggling out of it— like ripping a Band-Aid off. She was naked and he was staring.

Oh. She was naked.

And he was staring.

He sank onto the bed, nostrils flared, lips parted, inspecting every inch of her while gripping the edge of the bed with white-knuckled fists. "I want to touch you," he ground the words out.

She could breathe again, barely. "I'd like that."

"Gwen." He held his hand out to her, taking hers and pulling her forward until she was standing between his legs. His gaze followed the path of his hands, along her sides, down her forearms, the flare of her hips and around. The trail of his fingers, the barest whisper of a touch, had her arching into him.

His lips pressed the hollow between her breasts, open-mouthed and warm against her skin. A ragged groan slipped from his mouth as his hand came up to cup the weight of her breast. His thumb traced the nipple, sending shockwaves of sensation along her skin. When his mouth replaced his thumb, Gwen's hands tangled into his hair, desperate, against him.

Lam was a giving lover. His hands were firm, work-roughened but gentle. From the swell of her rear to the juncture at her thighs, he was deliberate and unhurried in his exploration. Hands and mouth, fingers and tongue, he had her breathless and frantic.

She gave as good as she got. Discovering the plans and angles of his stomach. The ripple and shift of the muscles in his back. The slight scrape of his stubble under her lips and the taste of his skin. Lam's moans, the tightening of his hands in her hair and the feel of his mouth on her breast…letting go had never been so exhilarating.

When he rolled her beneath him, she fumbled with the button and zipper of his jeans, pushing his jeans and boxers aside. She reached down, stroking the length of his erection and pulling another groan from deep in his chest. Hearing him, feeling him jerk against her hand was deeply empowering. Lam wanted her.

He clasped her wrist and lifted her hand, kissing her palm, her wrist before releasing her.

"You're beautiful, Gwen," he whispered, nudging between her legs. The fire in his eyes burned away any lingering doubts.

The way he looked at her made her feel beautiful. She ran her hands down his back and hooked one leg around his hips. Asking, pleading. The precious seconds it took for him to find and don a condom only ratcheted up her hunger for him.

His jaw was rigid when he moved, slowly, inside of her. She'd known it would be different, but not like this. The sweet pressure of his invasion forced the air from her lungs and threw off her center of gravity. It was incredible.

She was breathing hard and straining against him when his gaze locked with hers. He paused, then slid out before thrusting even deeper.

The noise she made was raw, startled, broken, mingled with his.

The slide of him, over and over, grew more potent with each thrust. Holding on to him, gazes locked, kept Gwen locked in pure sensation. His hands smoothed her hair from her face as he bent to kiss her, matching the slide of his tongue with the thrust of his body.

His arms held her close as he flipped them over. And the smile on his face was one of pure pleasure.

Chapter Eleven

S HE WAS INCREDIBLE. Wide-eyed, staring down at him, realizing she was in control.

He wanted to remember this. Every second.

Her long hair falling down her back and over her shoulders. And her body. Damn, her body. He'd gladly spend the rest of the night mapping out her every dip and curve if it meant he could dedicate it to memory. Her sighs and moans threatened the control he was clinging so tightly to. Every stroke of her hand, brush of her mouth…he was fighting a losing battle.

And when she began moving, one hand bracing herself against his chest, he was sure he was done. Her abandon rolled her on top of him, arching harder, faster, deeper, pushing him closer to the edge. He watched her, his hands tightening on her hips, encouraging her—holding her, needing her. Making love to her was the most powerful experience of his life.

Her eyes flew open as her body shuddered hard, her muscles clamping down on him, as his name spilled from her lips, over and over. He came apart then, lost in her eyes, her passion, and her body. She caught his moan in her kiss, cradling his face in her hands as his climax left him spent.

"Damn, woman," he groaned, wrapping an arm around

her and holding her against his chest.

She laughed, still breathless, and buried her face against his chest. "Damn, man."

He chuckled then, running his fingers along her back.

"Where is your family?" she asked. "I only ask because I might have been a little loud."

"Other hallway," he murmured. "As long as you're not screaming, we should be good."

"For a minute there, I wasn't sure." She laughed.

The idea of her screaming in pleasure had a certain appeal. "I'll have to work harder next time."

She looked all rumpled and flushed and gorgeous. "I'm not sure I'd survive it if you work harder."

"Guess we'll have to see." He ran his fingers through her hair.

She studied him closely, her gaze wandering over his neck and shoulders and chest. She was nibbling her lower lip as she held his hand up, turning it in the light and resting it on the blanket.

"Done?" he asked.

She shook her head and sat up, continuing her inspection of his southerly parts. Her brows rose high.

"You're next," he murmured.

Her gaze flew back to his face. "You already had your turn."

"Are there some sort of rules I don't know about?" he asked, loving her smile.

"You'd probably know better than I would." She tucked a curl behind her ear, her gaze falling from his.

Because she'd only slept with the ass that left her. And,

dammit, if he could undo some of the damage the bastard had done to her, he was going to try. "Don't get shy on me now." He rolled onto his side, propping himself up on his elbow. "It's definitely not allowed."

She shot him that saucy grin he loved.

"That." He pointed at her face. "That smile *is* allowed. And encouraged."

She laughed. "I think you're making these up as you go."

"And your laugh." That had rapidly become one of his favorite sounds.

She tilted her head. "Lam?" Her tone was soft. Uncertain. But she stopped herself before she could say anything else.

He waited, hoping she'd open up to him.

"I should go." She arched her back then stretched her arms up and over her head.

The movement did interesting things to her body. And even more interesting things to his. "Now?" he asked, already reaching for her.

Her gaze slid down, widened, before she jumped on him. "After."

He was laughing then, a deep belly laugh.

"Lam, shh." She pressed a hand over his mouth.

As his laughter subsided, he pressed a kiss against her fingertips.

She shook her head, still smiling as she kissed him.

He pulled her beneath him this time, sealing his lips to hers as he slid deep inside of her. Her cry was raspy and wavering and sexy as hell.

If she was leaving, he'd make sure she left here thinking

of him. He loved her with everything he had. And when she was biting into his pillow, he slid his fingers between them and stroked her until she was screaming into his pillow. He followed her over the edge, holding on to her as his release crashed into her.

Minutes later, they were still breathless and gasping, tangled up in each other and dozing. What would it be like to wake up beside her? To have the same heavy-lidded smile she was giving him now greet him first thing in the morning?

His fingers threaded with hers. "Stay. I'll wake you up in a few hours."

"I want to, but…" She shook her head. "If the girls wake up and I'm not there, it won't be pretty. I shouldn't have stayed as long as I have." She rolled onto her back, stared up at the ceiling, and smiled. "Bet you can't guess what I'm thinking."

He chuckled. He had no idea. She kept him guessing. But he knew what he wanted so why not put it out there. "You can't wait for tomorrow night?"

She turned her head to look at him, brows high. "I was thinking about that thing you did with your fingers."

"You keep that up and you're not leaving anytime soon."

Her gaze darted down.

"Give me five minutes." He laughed.

"You want me to come back tomorrow night?"

Was she uncertain because she honestly didn't see how much he wanted her here? Or because she wasn't sure she wanted to come back?

He leaned over her, looked her straight in the eye, and said, "Whenever you want, I want you here." He swallowed.

"I guess I'm getting partial to having you around. Incredible sex aside."

She shot him a saucy smile and slipped from his bed. He groaned and fell forward, face-first, into her pillow. It smelled like her. He breathed deep.

"Where is my pajama top?" she asked.

He looked up but didn't see her. Leaning over the edge of the bed revealed her on her hands and knees, peering under his bed. It was quite a view. "Take my shirt."

She sat up. "And my explanation for wearing your shirt?"

"You couldn't find your pajama top after seducing me and, since I didn't think it was okay for you to walk through the halls naked, I loaned you my shirt."

She rolled her eyes, but laughed.

They found her top. While he was pulling on his clothes, she wandered around his room, pausing every now and then.

"Who is this cutie?" she asked, holding Grant's picture. "What a smile."

He was used to the pain, but that didn't make it any easier. "That's Grant. My son." He forced the words out.

She froze, staring at the picture, then beyond, at the others. Every one of them was his boy. From babyhood to his sixth birthday. Smiling and laughing, fishing and covered in mud. Every treasured image holding together what was left of his heart.

Until now.

Now…he wanted her to know about his boy. Wanted to talk about him, with Gwen.

"He died four years ago." He cleared his throat. "Bee sting. We didn't know he was allergic."

Gwen was staring at him, his son's photo pressed to her chest.

"I don't talk about him." He shook his head. "I wasn't there."

Tears were running down her cheeks.

"I was there when he was born. For his first tooth, first steps, first day of school. But the one time he needed me, I wasn't there. I was at a cattle auction, in Houston—work. If I'd been here…" He kept shaking his head. "It seems wrong. I can't come to terms with that."

She put the photo back on the shelf with heartbreaking tenderness then launched herself at him. Her arms wound around his waist. It wasn't a gentle hug—it was fierce and hard, just like the sobs coming from her chest. There was no apology in her tears, no excuses for the grief she was feeling.

Her grief tore at him. Raw and loud and real.

When Grant died, his family thought they were doing a kindness by hiding their grief from him. "No one talks about him." His words were hoarse. "They don't want to hurt me. But not talking about him, whispering about him, is worse. It's like he never existed." His voice broke. Memories of Grant rushed in on him, filling his heart with so much love. "But he did. I don't want to forget the way he'd smile when I came through the door. Or how he hunted high and low until he had the same straw hat I had. He couldn't whistle but he loved to sing—not that he was much good at it." His voice was thick now, the words a rush. "He was my boy."

Until now, he'd kept his grief and his tears bottled up. She gave him permission to let go. Gwen's hold didn't ease. Not when she led him back to the bed or lay down at his side. She stayed and listened, holding him tight, while he shared his son with her.

GWEN HAD BEEN watching Lam sleep for the last hour. She'd never hurt for someone like this. Her girls were her life, her world. She refused to think about the sort of suffering he'd been through. No parent would willingly go there.

She'd been worrying about calling Dominic—dealing with whatever drama he'd surely throw her way. But this…this was real and horrible and overwhelming.

How could he get up every day? Function? Breathe?

All she knew was he needed her, desperately. Her mother would tend to the girls, if they woke up and found her gone. Chances were, her mother would know exactly where she was. She hadn't missed the side-long look she and Mrs. Draeger had exchanged.

Not that she relished the idea of sneaking from his room and running into one of the Draegers. It was four thirty-three. If she waited much longer, there was a good chance someone would see her. She took care to slide from the bed, hoping he'd sleep a bit longer. Last night had been exhausting for her—she could only imagine how he'd feel in the morning.

She lingered by the photos of Grant Draeger, etching the boy into her heart. On impulse, she picked up Lam's shirt and hugged it close. She needed the comfort of his scent and, since she couldn't take him with her, his shirt would have to do.

No one caught her. The girls were piled up, sound asleep. Her mother's snores were audible from outside her bedroom. Instead of running the risk of waking one of her girls, a forty-minute nap in the recliner sounded good. But once she'd stopped moving, thoughts of Lam, his boy, and the chasm of grief he dealt with regularly had her crying again. What she wouldn't do to ease his suffering. It was wrong, he was right. No one should lose a child. Now she understood the horrible, inescapable reason behind his anguish.

Eventually, she cried herself to sleep. When she woke a couple of hours later, she showered, dressed, and headed into the kitchen to face another day.

Today was the big day. Wedding day.

She'd planned ahead as much as possible, for the family meals and the catering. Priscilla's five-tier Chantilly crème-and-berry cake layers were ready to be iced and assembled, with sugar crystal flowers and hearts.

Priscilla and her soon-to-be-husband, Willie, wanted a wide variety of options for appetizer hour. Shot glasses of tomato soup with mini grilled cheese bites. Prosciutto wrapped figs with goat cheese. Flatbread. Oysters, stuffed mushrooms, and a sampling of skewers—fruit, vegetable, meat, and donuts.

Fresh green salad and Tuscan crusted rolls.

The main courses? Red snapper. Quail. And filet mignon.

The chocolate chip banana muffins, peach pecan twists, and breakfast casserole were ready and, on the table, when the Draeger family started gathering.

Lam was the last one to arrive, looking surprisingly well rested and more devastatingly handsome than ever. Probably because she knew how he looked when he was naked. How amazing it felt to have his skin pressed against hers. Or how incredible he was with his hands.

More than that, she knew the depths of this man's love. After Dominic, and her father had left, she'd begun to wonder if a father's love differed from a mother's. Lam Draeger had proven her wrong.

"Morning." His slow smile almost had her pouring coffee in his lap and not his mug.

"Morning."

"Big day." Macon served his mother and sister some casserole. "Ready?"

She nodded, tearing her attention from Lam and flipping through her lists. "Ready."

"Most of the servers will be arriving about an hour before start time, but I've enlisted a couple of boys to come out earlier to help with set up." Tabby smiled. "Not that you need to worry about that part."

To Gwen's relief, Tabby only expected her to cook. Serving and set up was Tabby's domain. Cleanup would be a communal event.

"We can help," Lam offered.

"I'll take you up on it." And later, if she wasn't too exhausted, she would take him up on his other offer.

Macon nodded. "Yep. I'll put on my dancing boots, too. You know what they say about tipsy bridesmaids."

The table fell instantly quiet, all eyes on Macon.

"I'm ashamed of you, Macon." Tabby shook her head.

"How old are you?"

Gwen was too flustered to sit, until Lam glanced her way, then at the empty seat between him and Jilly. She smiled, nodded, and took her seat.

"You need to eat," he murmured while reaching for a muffin.

She nodded, cutting up Amy's and Jilly's casserole and splitting a muffin between them. Before she'd had time to serve herself, Lam had filled her plate. She shot him a grin, the grin he liked, and was rewarded by his hand, sliding beneath her skirt and behind her knee. When he had kissed her there, she had had to bury her face in pillows to stay quiet.

She stepped on his foot. His well-protected boot-wearing foot.

He laughed.

"What's so funny?" Mrs. Draeger asked. "You're looking mighty pleased with yourself this morning, Lambert."

He had every right to look that way. He'd earned it. Gwen couldn't look at him. Or anyone else. She stared, intently, at her pecan peach twist.

"Guess I woke up on the right side of the bed." He shrugged and ate with enthusiasm.

"What's wrong side?" Amy was perplexed.

"No." Lam shook his head. "It's a saying. Silly."

Amy blinked, wrinkling her little face in confusion.

Lam sat back in his chair and scratched his chin. "You know, Amy, I'm not sure why people say things that mean something else. What it means is, I woke up happy."

"Oh." Amy smiled. "Me too."

"Me too too," Jilly added. "Fairy huntin' 'morrow."

Gwen nodded. "Right. *After* everyone is gone." Her attention wandered back to her lists.

It was one of the longest days of her life. Thankfully, her mother and Mrs. Draeger took the girls into town for lunch and some shopping.

Macon and Lam were as good as their word, pulling things out of ovens, washing pans or utensils, or offering words of encouragement. Lam's quick kiss in the pantry was one of the highlights of her day. The man could kiss.

But she cut things short and got back to work, arranging a tray with handmade chocolates when Lam held the phone out. "Phone call."

Gwen stared at it, momentarily terrified. "Who—who is it?"

Lam's jaw clenched, his brow furrowed. "It's Tabby, Gwen. Here." He put the phone on speaker, his searching gaze fixed on her.

"Gwen? You there? You have to come over in about ten minutes." Tabby's voice rang out. "Priscilla and Willie want to introduce you."

"I thought I was remaining strictly behind the scenes." She shot Lam a worried look.

He was still staring, studying her. He knew something was up.

"You're telling me the chef doesn't come out when patrons want to meet them and thank them for their meal?" Tabby's voice was muffled by the background noise.

"Not as often as the movies would like you to believe," she quipped, earning a laugh from Lam and Macon.

"Gwen," Tabby pleaded.

"Fine. Ten minutes." She stared down at her pale blue dress. "I'm going to need every one of them."

"We got this," Macon offered, his elbows deep in soap suds.

With a quick nod, Gwen hurried to her room. With a few twists and clips, she perfected her nineteen forties victory rolls. Her peach body-hugging number with a flare at the knees was her best-looking dress, so she tugged it on. Platform two-tone Mary Janes and stockings with the seam up the back finished the outfit. She kept her makeup fresh, but added her signature eyeliner and a splash of red lipstick. Nine minutes and forty-nine seconds.

She hurried back to the kitchen.

"Bad idea." Lam was wiping his hands on a dish towel.

She looked down at her dress. "What? Why?" It was old. Was it torn or stained?

"Brides don't like to be upstaged on their big day." He tossed the dish towel on the counter.

"He has a point, Gwen. You look mighty fine." Macon nodded.

Was it wrong that she liked the way Lam scowled at his brother? "Don't you have some drunk bridesmaids to track down?"

Macon laughed. "Yeah, sure. I'll walk you over there, Gwen."

"We can all go." Lam unrolled his shirtsleeves. "If you think we're presentable?"

Gwen made a big show out of inspecting them. But the Draeger men would look good in a paper bag. They wore starched black jeans, black boots, and white, pressed shirts. Traditional, respectful, and perfectly acceptable attire for a barn wedding. Even one as over-the-top expensive as this one was.

"Guess it'll have to do." She smiled. "A quick in and out, though, okay?"

"Sounds good." Lam held out his arm. "I have some work to do later." The sparkle in his eyes told her exactly what he meant—and had her missing a step, but he steadied her.

"Live a little," Macon said, leading the way.

"Is it hard work?" she asked, her voice low as they crossed the deck and stepped down onto the path.

"Hardest yet, I'm thinking." He glanced after his brother before stealing a quick kiss. "You look gorgeous."

"Says the man who's hoping to get lucky." She nudged him.

"I've been feeling pretty lucky since you and the girls showed up."

Chapter Twelve

"YOU OKAY?" TABBY asked for the eighth time. "You don't have to hang out, you know?"

Lam nodded, doing his best to look like he wasn't watching Gwen. They'd arrived and Tina had swept her across the room to two suit-wearing men, who were openly assessing her.

"They're producers," Tabby explained. "I guess Willie's family is in television. Tina showed them Gwen's tape." She shrugged. "She's got that thing, you know? A spark?"

He knew. "They want to put her on TV again?"

"I'm not sure." She frowned. "Guess that would sort of mess things up for you two, wouldn't it?"

Lam didn't answer.

Gwen was laughing at something one of the men said, her head bent low so she could hear.

Last night had been incredible, but nothing had been established between them. She didn't know how much he loved her. And, if whatever she was talking about with these television producers led to something good for her, she'd never know. He wasn't going to stand in her way. He knew all too well how fleeting happiness could be.

She was one hell of a cook. A chef, really. Watching her in the kitchen was awe-inspiring. If he believed in magic, he could use that as an explanation for her way with flavors and food. But that would also imply she wasn't somehow responsible for the food she created. It was all Gwen. Period. She had a gift.

If he was being honest with himself, she was too talented for Last Stand. There's no way this is what she'd imagined when she'd pictured her future. Hell, she'd only come back here because she'd had no choice.

"I'm gonna head back." He forced a smile for his sister. "You did good, you know that?"

"Of course." Tabby did a little bow. "Thank you."

Lam headed back down the path to the main house, the music and conversation from the wedding fading with every step. But the quiet didn't last long. Marta, his mother, and the girls were back from town.

"Look, Cowboy-Man," Jilly squealed when he walked into the kitchen. She stomped her little booted feet. "Like you."

Lam nodded and squatted beside her. "Those are some mighty fine looking boots, Jilly Bean." He smiled. "You're a real cowgirl now."

Jilly flung her arms around his neck. "They're brown, like yours," she whispered.

Her sweet words wrapped themselves around his heart. He scooped her up, standing. "Brown is the best color for boots." From the corner of his eye, he saw Amy. In gray boots. "Or gray. If you didn't get brown, you'd have to get gray, Jilly."

Amy came running then. "Like me."

Lam squatted again, making her spin so he could see the

boots from every angle. "Yes, ma'am. Those boots are the prettiest gray boots a cowgirl could have."

Amy took a few steps closer but stopped short of hugging him.

He scooped her up in his other arm and carried them across the kitchen. "I think we need snacks."

Marta was smiling. "We do?"

"Amy said something about a fairy movie?" he asked, remembering how excited the little girl had been at the breakfast table.

"Really?" Amy asked, stunned. "Really, Cowboy-Man?"

He nodded. "Yup."

"Yay." Jilly clapped her hands.

"You're going to watch a fairy movie?" His mother's shock was obvious.

"I can't think of a single thing I'd rather do tonight." He nodded. "How about some pretzels? And chocolate milk?"

"Well, now, I think we can do that." Marta nodded. "I might just have to join you."

"Wings," Amy said, tapping his shoulder. "Wings."

"Down, peez." Jilly nodded.

"You two go get your wings." Marta patted their little backs.

They ran, their boots clapping against the wooden floor.

He smiled. "That's a familiar sound. Remember Grant? In his first pair of boots?" He waited, acting like it was everyday he mentioned the topic they all took such great pains to avoid.

"I do." There was a slight quiver in Marta's voice. "He was so proud of those boots. We had to wait until he was sleeping to take them off."

Even then, Lam had made sure to put them right by Grant's bed. Because real cowboys always kept their boots nearby.

"I do." His mother sniffed. "But, oh—" She broke off, pressing a hand to her mouth. "You were spinning him around. You remember? And you'd just bought those news boots, a little too big." She laughed. "That boot went flying so hard and fast, it's a wonder your brother didn't lose an eye."

He hugged his mother, kissed her cheek, and headed to the pantry. "Pretzels." He grabbed the bag and headed out. "Chocolate milk?"

"What are we doing?" Macon asked.

"I don't know what you're doing? Something to do with bridesmaids?" He shot his brother a look.

"Macon." His mother clicked her tongue.

"It was a joke." He sat at the counter. "Seriously, what are we doing?"

"Movie night," Lam said.

"Popcorn?" Macon asked.

"If you make it." Lam shrugged.

Macon slid off the stool and headed into the pantry while Lam poured out three glasses of milk.

"You know, Lam, we still have some of his toys and things boxed up." His mother paused. "If you're ready, maybe the girls could use some of it?"

"They didn't come with much." Marta nodded. "I need to take Gwen shopping. You should see the state of her underwear." She broke off with a look at Lam. "Not you, of course."

Lam held up his hands. He could say, in all honesty, that he'd never seen her in her underwear.

"Has she said what happened?" Mrs. Draeger asked.

Lam listened, pouring a healthy dose of chocolate into each glass of milk.

Macon opened the popcorn pack and put it in the microwave, then leaned against the counter.

Marta shrugged. "Not much. My girl. Her pride is important to her. But I heard her, early this morning, crying."

Lam paused. She hadn't been crying over the man who'd left her, he was certain of that. When she spoke of him, there was no wistfulness, only regret. No, her tears were for his boy and his grief, and it filled his heart.

"I know they'd moved around a lot. Some places not so good. He left her without any money, phone, food, nothing. She would have been on the street if their neighbor hadn't taken them in. What sort of person does something like that?" Marta broke off. "I found this in her laundry. I can't help but read some sort of threat into it."

Lam took the crumpled letter Marta held out. The letter Gwen had been staring at, white-faced, that day. He read the words and saw red. "If I ever meet this man, I'm not sure he'll walk away without permanent injury." He opened his mouth, then closed it, because everyone in the kitchen was staring at him.

"Is he a threat to Gwen?" Macon asked.

"Not so long as she's here." Lam stared at the number. Gwen wouldn't thank him for getting involved. If she'd wanted him to know, she'd have told him. But he couldn't sit by and do nothing. What if this man tried to win her back? Would she go? He didn't think so—but he might be seeing things the way he wanted them to be.

"You're sweet on her, aren't you?" his mother asked.

"Just because I think her ex is an ass doesn't mean I'm sweet on anyone." He shot Macon a look. "I like Gwen well enough. She deserves to be happy."

"So do you." His mother sighed. "I was hoping one of you would marry her, keep her and those precious girls right here with me."

"Our kids are too old to boss around now, I guess." Marta laughed.

"Are you making some for me?" his mother asked. "I'm partial to chocolate milk."

"You're partial to chocolate." Lam grinned and pushed one of the glasses her way.

"Wings," Jilly declared, wearing a set and holding more out. "For you and you and you and you."

Lam stopped stirring. "I don't want to break them, Jilly."

"They have elastic straps," his mother pointed out. "They stretch."

"Yup, Ade-lady." Jilly pulled the straps.

"Ade-what-now?" Macon asked.

"You can't expect them to call me Mrs. Draeger, now, can you?" She sipped her chocolate milk. "I'll take some."

Jilly offered her a pair of glittery wire wings.

"Ade-lady," Macon repeated. "I want a name. What's my name?"

Jilly and Amy looked at each other. "Laffy," Amy said.

"Cuz you laugh," Jilly said.

Lam laughed himself at that.

"And that's Gramma. And Cowboy-Man." Jilly held out wings as she spoke.

"I'll take a pair," Macon said. "Laffy's not so bad. I can think of worse names to call someone. I've got a choice few for you right now," he said, shooting Lam a pointed look.

"Names we will not use in the presence of fairy princesses." Their mother used her firm voice.

"Wait, what are we watching?" Macon asked, playing with the straps of his wings.

"*The Magical Fairy Princesses*," Amy said.

"Of course." Macon smiled. "Make me one of those." He nodded at the chocolate milk. "Gwen have anything sweet stashed anywhere?"

She had. A Chantilly crème-and-berry super-sized cupcake, just for him. She'd put it in the back of the fridge in a white paper box.

"I think there are some oatmeal raisin cookies in the cookie jar." Marta glanced at him. "Your favorite."

"Yes, he's her favorite." Macon sighed. "Twice he's gotten chicken fried steak. Pot roast once. Now cookies."

"Momma's nice." Amy smiled.

"She is," Macon agreed. "I wouldn't mind her being as nice to me as she is to Lam, is all. I mean, Cowboy-Man."

Lam knew exactly what he meant. "Make your own chocolate milk."

"I'm pretty sure you'll make me a glass," Macon said, crossing his arms over his chest. "Did I tell you what I saw the other morning, Mom?"

Lam pulled a glass from the cabinet, slammed it on the

counter and poured the milk.

"Lambert. Careful you don't break something." His mother shook her head. "What did you see?"

Lam stirred the spoon quickly, making sure to make as much noise with the spoon as possible.

Macon was doubled over with laughter.

"I swear, you boys and your secret little jokes." Their mother stood. "Let's get this movie set up, fairy princesses."

"Thanks." Macon grabbed his glass, a large bowl of popcorn, and followed them from the kitchen.

"You're good with them." Marta stacked oatmeal raisin cookies on a plate.

"They're sweet girls."

"I worry about Amy and how shy she is." Marta nodded. "Jilly seems to make up for it. The only one who seems troubled by where they came from is Gwen." She smiled at him. "It's hard. As a parent, all you want is for your child to be happy."

He nodded. "I get the feeling she's still figuring out what that looks like for her." Having Dominic back in the picture was likely to complicate that. But Gwen was strong, resilient—she'd figure it out. He only hoped she knew she wasn't in this alone.

"And you?" She patted his hand. "Have you figured out what makes you happy?"

He stared into his chocolate milk, the answer on the tip of his tongue. It was two wing-and-boot wearing little girls and their incredible mother. They made him happy. Having them here, made him happy. "I'm working on it."

She shook her head. "Well, you can work on it later.

Right now, we're eating cookies and watching fairies." She nodded. "Don't you forget your wings."

"Yes, ma'am."

GWEN WALKED ALONG the path to the back door, her heels swinging from her finger. She wanted a nice, hot shower and a long, deep sleep.

And Lam.

But if she took a shower and went to see Lam, sleeping wasn't likely to happen.

She opened the back door, smiling at the kitchen's pristine state. One less thing she had to do. It was late, so the girls would be in bed—thanks to her mother.

Now all she had to do was decide what she wanted more? Sleep or Lam?

It wasn't a difficult decision. She headed through the kitchen and into the main house, making a beeline for his room. But she came to a screeching halt at the site that greeted her.

Her mother and Mrs. Draeger were sleeping.

Macon was propped on one elbow, staring blankly at the television screen.

Lam sprawled on the couch, also sleeping, Amy draped over one leg, Jilly propped up on the other. They, too, were sleeping. It was, without a doubt, the sweetest thing she'd ever seen. He was amazing.

"Are you wearing wings?" she whispered to Macon, giggling.

He shrugged. "Don't hate on the wings."

She covered her mouth now, his deadpan delivery too much.

"What did I miss?" Lam stirred, wincing when he realized the girls were using him for a bed. She couldn't blame them.

"Our wings. She thinks it's hilarious. I'm offended." Macon stood, stretched, and slid off his wings. "I'm gonna head into town, see if I can find a pool game. Wanna come?"

"Me?" she asked, surprised.

"You? Lam? The girls?" Macon shrugged, smiling. "It was a joke. I'm pretty sure you two already have plans." He winked, handed her the wings, and headed for the front door.

"Need help?" She reached for Amy. "Looks like you had a good time."

He nodded, holding Jilly as he stood. "Nothing like a fairy princess party and chocolate milk to make it really feel like Saturday night."

"You Draeger boys are all feisty tonight." She led the way back through the kitchen, down the hall to her mother's apartment, and into the room she was sharing with her girls.

He lay Jilly on the bed, carefully removing her wings and shoes.

"Is she wearing boots?" Gwen asked.

"The mothers took them shopping." He nodded. "You're all sleeping here?"

She nodded, removing Amy's wings and boots. "Better than a sofa and some sleeping bags." She smoothed the blankets over the girls and stood beside Lam in the dark.

His hand reached for hers. She draped his arm over her shoulders and leaned into his side. "You were amazing today."

"You weren't so bad yourself."

"Yeah, tasting food and carrying things is tough." He lips brushed her temple.

It was the lightest of touches, almost instinctual, and it touched her. "We should let them sleep."

They tiptoed out of the room and closed the door behind them.

"What now?" he asked.

"I'm starving," she admitted.

"Glad I made you eat something this morning now, aren't you?" His grin was a little smug and a whole lot adorable.

"I am, thank you." Her hand caught his as they headed back into the kitchen. "Are you hungry?"

"If you're cooking, I'm not saying no." He followed her. "How about we make something together?"

She stood on tiptoe to kiss him.

"Keep that up and food will have to wait," he murmured against her lips. "You wanna tell me about the letter?"

"My mom?" she asked.

"In the laundry," he said, his hands stroking up and down her arms.

She shook her head. "Nope. I don't want to talk about it." But she did. She wanted to share it with him. And it scared her.

"Is he going to cause problems?"

"I don't know. I need to call him…" She swallowed. "I

guess."

"After we talk to a lawyer." He tipped her chin back. "If you want?"

She stared up at him, willing to stay this way. Close, touching, together. He wanted to help her. There was no way she'd turn him down. "Yes, please."

He exhaled, his posture easing. "Good. Now food."

With a sigh, she went back to searching the refrigerator. "Snapper? Too much work." She pulled out a few plastic storage bins. "Why cook when we can warm stuff up?"

He leaned against the counter, watching as she arranged berries, some leftover breakfast casserole, a biscuit and some clotted cream on a plate. "You make it look too pretty to eat."

She popped a blueberry into her mouth. "More for me."

The kitchen door swung open and her mother came in, yawning. "You eating?" she asked, not pausing as she made her way through the kitchen. "See you two in the morning. Your mother went to bed, too. Get some sleep, Gwen. Don't you keep her up late, Lam. You hear me?"

"Yes, ma'am," Lam nodded. "I think she knows."

"Lam, it's possible everyone knows." And she wasn't upset. Which was a surprise.

"Well, if that's the case, how about we go out for dinner?" He smoothed some chocolate spread on a biscuit.

She smiled. "Really?" What would that be like?

He paused. "Last Stand's small, but we could actually go out."

"On a date?" Was he serious?

"That's normally what single people do." He nodded and

took a bite of his biscuit, a dollop of chocolate on the corner of his mouth. "This could be a problem." He held up the biscuit.

"That's supposed to be for your mother." She laughed, reaching over to wipe the chocolate from his mouth.

He caught her hand and pressed a kiss to her palm. "And, yes, I was serious."

"What would we do, on this date?" She squeezed his hand.

He shrugged. "I don't know. It's been awhile." He opened the fridge, pulled out another biscuit, and popped it into the microwave.

"You haven't dated since your divorce?"

He stopped the microwave before it beeped and carried his plate back to the counter. "I wasn't interested."

"And now you are?" She popped the elastic band on the wings he was still wearing.

He laughed, shrugging them off and tossing them onto the counter. "In dating?" He shook his head. "In you?" He stood there, hands shoved in his pockets, staring at her. He didn't say a word. He didn't have to. The look on his face said it all.

What scared her was the longing he stirred. Not just in her body, but in her heart.

To say she and Dominic had had a dysfunctional relationship was an understatement. But when she was in it, she'd held on—especially once the girls were involved. But things like mutual respect and companionship, sharing a laugh or a story? That hadn't been part of it. He'd been the chef, she'd been his sous chef. Always beneath him. Always learning from him. Always subject to his criticism or berating or demeaning. What they'd had wasn't love.

None of that existed with Lam. What did exist was more potent and real. *If* she loved him, she risked being broken in a way she wasn't sure she'd recover from. Because she'd done more than share her body with him. She'd shared her wounds and her fears, and he hadn't flinched. Because that's what people who truly loved each did. They loved each other, imperfections, scars, insecurities, and all.

"Eat." He stroked her cheek. "I'll be back."

She nodded, the pang in her heart blossoming into something more. Something impossible to ignore. She sat, pulling the wings out from under her. He'd been wearing *wings*, for crying out loud.

For her girls.

She held the wings close.

Lam Draeger.

Being in love with him meant staying here. Raising the girls here. With her mother. And his family. The girls would be thrilled. So would Jax.

Assuming he loved her, too, and this wasn't just some passing fancy. She nibbled a berry and poked the casserole. Today had been long and exhausting—too exhausting to be considering life-altering decisions. Not that there was anything left to consider.

She loved him. Lambert Draeger had her heart. And instead of fear or worry, she felt joy and hope. Because of Lam.

He appeared, a bottle of champagne in his hand. "We should celebrate. Tonight was a success. For Tabby, for the ranch, and for you."

"I'll toast to that." She was so flustered, she spun around and pretended to look for a corkscrew. Knowing she loved him was one thing. Telling him, opening herself up for rejection, was another.

With a deep breath, she turned to face him. He was already opening the bottle.

"I got it," he said, pouring them both a glass, and offering her one. "To..."

"Being happy?" It was a breathless question. She was happy. He made her happy. Did he feel the same way? Was she brave enough to ask?

"I'll drink to that." He was studying her again, the corner of his mouth kicking up as he closed the distance between them.

"Cheers," she said, touching the rim of her glass to his and taking a sip. "Yummy." Crisp and fruity and refreshing. "Very yummy." She set her glass down and started pulling the pins from her hair.

He helped, sliding his fingers though her hair, kneading her scalp with strong fingers. "You don't get a headache from all your fancy knots and twists?"

"Sometimes." She sighed, resting her forehead on his chest. She could definitely get used to this. "But there's nothing worse than hair in your food and I'm not a fan of the hairnet. Call me vain."

He chuckled. "You might make the hairnet sexy."

"No one could make a hairnet sexy." She peered up at him, admiring the view of Lam smiling down at her. Honestly, he took her breath away. "But I appreciate the vote of confidence."

They stood in comfortable silence, wrapped up in each other, until she remembered. "I have some news."

His posture changed, stiffened—enough for her to notice. "Oh?"

"A job." She straightened enough to see his face, curious about the odd edge in his voice. "Another wedding, I mean."

"Here?"

She nodded. "But I did get asked if I'd be willing to fly to locations to cater."

His brows rose and his posture instantly eased. "That's not a bad deal. Fly off somewhere, cook, and come back home. Nice they recognize talent when they see...and taste it."

She smiled. "Maybe." The money was good—because, apparently, people were willing to spend way too much money on a wedding.

"Maybe?" He twisted her hair and draped it over her shoulder. "Home. Travel. Cooking. Sounds pretty ideal."

"I don't like the idea of being so far away from the girls." She shrugged. "Not yet, anyway. They've had so many changes in their lives recently." But it wasn't just the girls she didn't want to be away from. It was Lam. "But it's nice to have options."

"You're considering all your options?" He was pulling her against him again. "Meaning, staying here. With...us."

"Momma?" Amy stood in the doorway, rubbing her eyes. "Jilly sick."

Lam pressed a kiss to her forehead and let her go. "Jilly's sick?"

"Tummy." Amy rubbed her tummy.

"I'm coming," she said, scooping Amy up. "Say good night to Cowboy-Man."

"Night," Amy mumbled.

"Need help?" Lam asked.

She shook her head. "But thank you."

He nodded, smoothing Amy's curls. "Those options we were talking about? Promise me you'll talk to me before you make any decisions?" He touched her cheek.

She stood on tiptoe and pressed a quick kiss to his cheek. "I will."

Chapter Thirteen

S HE KNEW SOMETHING was wrong as soon as she opened her eyes. After hours of throwing up cookies and pretzels and popcorn, Jilly was sound asleep, sprawled across the bed. But Amy was not on the pallet of pillows and quilts Gwen had made for her. A glance at the clock told her it was barely three. Amy was an early riser, but never this early.

Chances were, she was in the bathroom.

But three minutes ticked by and no Amy.

She hurried to check the bathroom. It was empty. So was the rest of her mother's small apartment.

"Mom?" She knocked, pushing her mother's bedroom door wide. "Mom?"

Her mother sat up. "What's wrong?"

Jilly had been throwing up, so it made sense Amy would prefer sleeping somewhere else. Still, something felt off. Wrong. "Is Amy in here with you?" Her chest felt heavy and her lungs empty.

Her mother clicked on the bedside lamp. "No." She stood, tugging on a robe. "She's not in the bathroom?"

"I can't find her." Her voice was high and brittle.

"She can't have gone far—"

"Kitchen?" Gwen asked, already running down the hall that connected her mother's apartment to the kitchen.

"Amy?" she called. "Amy, no more hiding, honey." She flipped on lights, searching under the table and in the pantry, before running into the great room. Maybe she was watching her movie again?

Please, please, let her be watching her movie again.

The empty room kicked her into full panic mode.

She ran down the hall and knocked on Lam's door. "Lam. Lam, I can't find Amy."

He yanked the door open, wearing boxers and his boots. "Where have you looked?"

"Inside…the kitchen. All the places the girls play." She was already running back down the hall. "She was there when I went to bed. It hasn't been that long…"

He took her by the shoulders. "We'll find her, you hear me?"

She nodded.

In minutes, Lam had roused his family as well as the ranch hands. After a search of the house and barn turned up nothing, Lam paused. "The orchard?"

"She's scared of the dark," her mother argued.

"Fairies," Tabby groaned.

Gwen ran out the door, Lam at her heels, the beam of his flashlight swinging as he ran. It wasn't a short trip—beyond the event barn, past the wedding chapel, and halfway to the large windmill leading to the pastures below. Too far for a three-year-old to go alone, in the dark.

"Please be there," she whispered. "Please be there. Amy?"

"Amy?" Lam's voice was louder, stronger. "Amy, Pumpkin, where are you?" The hitch in his voice almost triggered tears.

"Amy?" Macon's voice joined them.

Gwen spun, holding her flashlight high, desperation mounting.

Tree by tree, they worked their way down the first row. Then the second. By the third, she was a wreck, numb and shaking. Amy was here. She had to be here. There was no place else to look.

"Hear that?" Lam said, holding his hand up.

She held her breath, absolutely still.

"Barking?" Macon asked.

"Jax," she and Lam said in unison.

Lam whistled, Jax barked, and they ran. On the fifth whistle, they found Jax. He wasn't moving, but was standing guard by her sleeping daughter. Amy was curled up in a tiny ball, wearing her wings and cowboy boots.

Gwen's legs gave out, and she sank to the ground, fighting back sobs. "Amy," she whispered, pressing a kiss to her daughter's cheek. "My little pumpkin pie?"

"Momma?" Amy yawned. "Did you see them? The fairies?"

"I didn't." She pulled her daughter into her arms. "Not tonight. Oh, Amy, you scared me. And Cowboy-Man and Macon. We were all out looking for you."

"Jax with me." Amy pointed at the dog.

"Good boy, Jax," Gwen said, smiling at the dog. "You're getting a nice big steak for breakfast."

"He a good, good boy," Amy agreed, resting her head on Gwen's shoulder.

"You got her?" Lam asked, helping her to her feet.

She nodded, relief and fear and adrenaline making her

shake. "I can't let her go."

He hugged them close. "It's okay, Gwen. You've got her."

"I know," she sniffed.

"Let's get back to the house." He kept his arm around her shoulders all the way back, guiding them down the path, up the porch stairs, and into the kitchen. "You're barefoot?" He asked once they were inside and under the bright lights.

Was she? She glanced down at her dirty, bloody feet. She hadn't been thinking about shoes—she'd been thinking about finding Amy. "I guess." Not that it mattered right now. "She needs to go to bed."

"Let me take her, Gwen." Macon stepped forward. "You need to get your feet looked after."

"I'm fine." She buried her nose in Amy's knotted golden-red curls.

"Gwendolyn Hobbs." Her mother's tone was sharp. "Your baby girl is home, safe and sound, and sleeping. Now *my* baby girl needs tending."

"I'll be careful," Macon offered. "Remember, the wings. I'm fairy princess approved."

She smiled.

Macon took Amy, Lam sat in the chair opposite her, and Tabby appeared with a first aid kit.

"It doesn't hurt," she assured them.

"You're in shock," Lam said, sponging her feet clean. Even though his hands were trembling, his touch was so gentle. And soothing.

"Here," Mrs. Draeger pressed a cup of hot chocolate into her hands. "Chocolate makes everything better."

She smiled. "Thank you." She stared around the kitchen. She knew most of the faces that had come running when she'd needed help, but not all. Not that it mattered. Every one of them had been out there looking for Amy, no questions asked, in the middle of the night. "Thank you all, so much. Believe me, she will get a talking-to tomorrow morning."

"Course, Miss Gwen," Old John said. "She's a little thing, though, so don't be too hard on her."

"Helps that your momma's makin' doughnuts," another man said.

"Eat as many as you want, Hugo. You too, John." Her mother was quick, whipping up the batter and frying up fresh doughnuts in no time—cinnamon and sugar sprinkled on while they were still warm. "Too late to go back to bed, so I might as well feed you all."

Lam poked at her foot. "Ow," she cried.

"A thorn." He looked at her, concern creasing his brow.

It was only then that she realized he was sitting in his boxer shorts and boots and she was wearing his button-up shirt, something she'd taken from the laundry because sleeping in it was as close to sleeping with Lam as she could get. After taking care of Jilly, it was the only thing she had to sleep in.

"Lam," she whispered.

"Drink your hot chocolate." He worked on her foot, pulling three thorns and one nasty looking cactus needle free. He rubbed her foot and ankle with a warm washcloth, his blue eyes searching hers long enough to make the world steady again. "Next."

She was doing okay until the last thorn. Lam kept apologizing, even though it wasn't his fault. When it was done, and her feet were clean and wrapped up, Lam held her feet in his lap. He sat staring at her for a long time, his hands gently massaging her ankles. All she wanted was to climb into his lap, to have him wrap his arms around her, and let him hold her until the fear was gone.

"Lam?" she whispered.

"She's okay, Gwen." He nodded, his jaw locking. "It's all okay now. Once you finish that, you need some sleep. Okay?"

"Okay," she whispered. "Thank you."

"You don't have to thank me, Gwen. Not ever." He stood, stared down at her, then walked out of the room.

Lam. If she could have gone after him, she would have. What had tonight been like for him? She'd been too distraught over Amy to think of anything other than finding her. Not that it would have changed a thing. She needed help and she knew he'd help her. He would always be there for her, no matter what, because he was a good man.

The man she loved.

She loved him. So, so much.

"Go to bed, Gwen. Sleep in my bed." Her mother kissed her forehead. "I've got breakfast covered this morning," she said.

"But—"

"No buts, missy." Her mother stood, hands on hips. "Sleep is in order. You promised Lam, I heard you. Now go on."

Fine. Now probably wasn't the time to go make awkward, and potentially embarrassing, declarations. Lam was just as worked up as she was. He loved her daughters, that much she knew. A couple of hours sleep would be good for both of them. And then, she was going to tell Lam exactly how she felt.

Apparently, a couple of hours of sleep was *exactly* what she needed. She didn't remember her head hitting the pillow or a single dream. But when she woke, it was with a sense of optimism. After a nice hot shower, she took care to dress with Lam in mind, and doubled up on fuzzy socks to protect her sore feet. She ran a hand over her foot, thoughts of Lam and Amy and what could have happened knocking the air from her lungs.

She was lucky. So damn lucky. Not only because they'd found Amy but because Lam loved her. That was why he looked at her the way he did. At least, she hoped with all her heart that was the reason.

With a final pep talk in the mirror, she shuffled down the hall to the kitchen. Her mother was there, with the girls and Tabby. The girls had made her a get-well card, covered in glitter and puppy paw prints and hearts.

"I sorry, Momma." Amy burst into tears. "So s-sorry."

"I know, Pumpkin." She held her daughter close. "You can't ever leave the house alone though, okay? Especially at night. I know you want to see the fairies, but we have to be safe about it."

"Okay, Momma." Amy sniffed. "I'm sorry."

She rocked her daughter, pressing kisses to her forehead and savoring her slight weight in her arms.

"Cowboy-Man gonna take me." Amy sniffed. "And

Jilly."

"I know he will." She smiled, her heart so full.

"Gwen, you got a phone call?" Her mother handed her a paper. "Tina somebody?"

"I bet she's calling about the show's air date." Tabby smiled. "Aren't you excited?"

She kept on rocking Amy. "Why don't you call her, Tabby? I'm not in the mood for small talk." Right now, this is all that mattered. This and finding Lam."

"You sure?" Tabby asked.

She nodded.

"Okay." Tabby took the number and phone and left the kitchen for her call.

"We made you food," Jilly said, carrying the plate to the table.

"Strawberry jam toast? My favorite." She kissed her girls.

"I butted it." Amy smiled, a red-nosed, wavering smile that tore at her heart.

"I jammed." Jilly pointed at the toaster. "Gramma did the toast."

"Thank you all."

"Here, sweetie." Her mother put a steaming cup of tea on the table. "Drink up. Today, you're taking a break."

"Mom, I'm fine." She waved away her arguments. "I worked in a crazy busy kitchen, pregnant with twins, until the end of my third trimester. I think I can handle cooking a family meal in fuzzy socks."

"Gwen." Tabby held out the phone. "This is sort of important."

Gwen set down her toast and took the phone. "Yes?"

"Gwen? Tina here. Listen, the guys and I were hoping you'd be willing to come out and do a test pilot."

"I'm sorry? What does that mean?" She made a face at Jilly.

"It means the network loved the footage we filmed and is interested in giving you a thirty-minute cooking show." She paused. "Your own show. Doing what you do. Looking like you do."

Gwen was speechless. Absolutely stunned.

"Gwen?" Tina laughed. "You there?"

"I'm here." She set Amy down, stood, and hurried out the back door for some privacy. "You're serious?"

"Totally. You have a unique look, Gwen. Almost a Jessica Rabbit meets Betty Boop in the kitchen. I told you. It's a hook. A selling point. Something that will make you stand out."

Was that a compliment?

"And your food? Come on, your food is incredible." Tina launched into all the perks—possible cookbooks and merchandise. Things Gwen had no interest in at the moment. Only one thing mattered.

"I'm not sure what to say, Tina. But I do have one question. Where will the show be filmed?"

"ALL I KNOW is Dad sent money every month," Lam explained to his gathered siblings. It was time to get this out in the open. "There was no stipulation in his will, no explanation, just the automatic withdrawal that would have kept going, no questions asked, if I hadn't looked over his finances."

"Did you stop it? Cut her off?" Macon asked.

"We don't know her situation. Who she is? How dependent she is on the money?" Lam shook his head. "I couldn't."

Kolton stared at the picture. "Who do *you* think she is?"

Lam shook his head. "I'm not a fan of the what-if game. I was going to hold off on telling you until I knew more, but Gwen convinced me this wasn't something for me to deal with alone."

"Damn straight." Macon nodded, taking the picture from Kolton. "She looks familiar. She looks like..." His gaze darted to Tabby.

Tabby shrugged, taking the pictures. "Wait. You know who this is?" She shook her head. "I don't understand."

"Who?" Kolton sat up.

"It's her." Tabby held it out. "Look at the picture. Really look at. This is Sam's girlfriend. Remember? But her name wasn't Veronica."

Lam was stunned. Sam's girlfriend? The one he'd gone to prison over?

"Ronnie?" Macon nodded, taking the picture. "That's why she looked familiar."

"That's part of it. I'm guessing this is Sam's daughter?" Kolton asked.

Lam sat back against his desk. "Maybe." He shook his head. His dad was a hard man, but he'd lived by his word. Knowing that lifted the horrible weight that had been pressing against his chest.

"That's a relief." Macon studied the pictures. "And a surprise. Dad was sending them money? Why? After what happened with Sam…"

"I'm just as surprised as you are." Lam didn't want to admit what he he'd been thinking about their father. But now they were facing a whole slew of new questions. "I wonder if Sam knows?" Sam's insistence on isolating himself made it impossible to answer that question.

"He could have a daughter and not know it?" Tabby frowned. "Kendra? We have to tell him about her. Somehow."

"Let's take this one step at a time, okay?" Lam asked. "Whatever we do now, we talk it out and do it, together."

"Mom needs to know," Tabby said.

"Agreed." Macon nodded. "This is her granddaughter."

"We don't know that." Kolton shook his head.

Tabby held the photo up so she and the picture of Kendra were side by side. "I'm willing to risk it."

"I need a favor. Before we do any of that, there's something important I need to do…" He paused. "First, Kolton."

Kolton perked up.

"I need to apologize." He ran a hand over his face.

"I can't wait to hear this." Kolton smiled.

His brother wasn't going to make this easy, not that he'd expected anything else. "I might have implied that getting involved with Gwen would be wrong because she is an employee."

"You didn't imply it; you said it." Kolton nodded. "And?"

"And since I'm planning on proposing to Gwen tonight,

I figured I should let you know."

Macon was up, clapping him on the back and giving him a big hug.

Tabby hugged him too, grinning ear to ear.

Kolton smiled. "I knew it. I knew it. There was something between you, some vibe-y thing."

"The whole television show thing is going to throw a wrench into things." Tabby sighed. "But I'm glad you're going to stick it out. I think Gwen's worth it."

"Television thing?" He hadn't seen Gwen since early this morning, when he'd been on the verge of losing it. This morning, with Amy, had put it all into perspective. He could no longer ignore that she belonged with him, that this was their home. He didn't want to hide it, he wanted the world to know. And if she wasn't ready, he'd wait until she was. Unless he wasn't what she wanted and leaving Last Stand was.

"Tina called her this morning. They want her to have her own show. I thought you knew…"

He toyed with the ring in his pocket.

"You can't let it stop you," Tabby urged.

He nodded. "I won't." But he wasn't so sure. All he knew was he had two little girls he'd promised to take fairy hunting, and he wasn't about to keep them waiting.

"You go get engaged. This can wait one more day," Tabby stared down at the pictures. Macon nodded. "Before we talk to Mom, we need to decide what we're saying."

Once they agreed, he headed to the kitchen—where his favorite fairy princess cowgirls were waiting.

"Cowboy-Man," Jilly squealed, dancing around him.

"You're here. You're here. You're here."

"I am?" he asked, laughing.

"Yes." Amy nodded, pushing against his legs. "I can see you."

He chuckled, doing his best not to look too obvious as he searched the kitchen for some sign of Gwen.

"She's not here," Marta said. "She heard you were going to the orchard and got a head start, since she's not moving all that fast."

"She shouldn't be walking around," he growled.

"Well, she was pretty insistent about finding you," Marta snapped. "Said she had something important to tell you."

The television show. It was important? That was answer enough, then, wasn't it? He'd find a way to be excited for her. He wanted her happy, that's all. "I heard."

Marta smiled. "Go on, the three of you. Don't forget your flashlights."

Jax was waiting on the porch for them, choosing to walk between the girls instead of at his side. Lam approved. His dog had grown just as protective of the girls as he had. Poor Jax would miss them, too.

And Marta.

Their absence would be felt by them all.

The thing about little girls, he didn't have to say much. The two of them were so full of excitement, they carried on the whole walk. From what fairies drank—dew—to what they were scared of—birds—he was astounded there was so much information about a creature that didn't exist.

With any luck, he'd give the girls their fairies.

"Momma," Jilly squealed.

Sure enough, Gwen sat on a blanket, an electric lantern at her side. "Did you think I was going to miss out on the fairies?" she asked. "Thank you for bringing them, Cowboy-Man." There was a smile in her voice.

"Hoping they'll make an appearance." He sat on the blanket beside her. "I don't know if you'll have fairies where you're going? But I didn't want the girls to miss out."

"Going?" Her sigh was more than a little irritated "You talked to Tabby? I wanted to talk to you first—"

"I'm happy for you, Gwen. If this is what you want, you should do it." He forced a smile.

She was staring at him, looking almost annoyed. He wasn't exactly thrilled at the moment, either.

"Momma, where the fairies?" Jilly asked.

Lam patted the blanket. "Have a seat." He stared around, hoping like hell this would work. "You, too, Amy."

The girls sat, and Jax flopped down on the edge of the blanket.

"This is nice," Gwen said. "Just us. Waiting for the fairies. Look up, girls, see all the stars through the trees?"

Jilly climbed into his lap.

Amy was perfectly content to lay beside Jax.

For a minute, the ache for this, for them, overwhelmed him. He didn't want them to leave. Didn't want to walk into the kitchen and not see the girls. Or miss Gwen's excitement and energy in the kitchen. The noise and laughter, wings and stories, sticky fingers and glitter... They'd filled a hole, one he wasn't eager to feel again. Now that he knew they were his family, how was he supposed to let them go?

"Ready?" Jilly asked.

"Yep," he whispered. "Turn out your lights."

With the lights out, a million stars lit the sky. Out here, the sky was endless.

"Where?" Jilly whispered.

"Keep looking," Lam whispered, flashing his flashlight a few, quick times.

They sat there, quiet, in the dark, waiting for something that might not come. He did it again, hoping the burst of light would entice some "fairies" for the girls. He was about to give up when Amy sat up.

"Look," Amy whispered. "Look, Jilly."

Lam saw the glow and sat back, smiling. With fireflies, there was no guarantee.

"It's prettiful," Jilly said. "Look Momma, it's a fairy."

"I see it, Jilly Bean. Isn't she beautiful?"

In the dark, Gwen's hand covered his and, damn his weakness, he held on. He'd be a fool not to savor every last second he had with them.

The fireflies stayed long enough to make the girls happy, so happy they chattered all the way back to the house. Gwen tried to keep up, but he could tell her feet were bothering her.

"Jilly, can you hold this?" He handed Jilly the electric lantern. "Hold it high so we can see, okay?"

"Got it." She held it high.

"Just like that." Without asking, he swung Gwen up into his arms.

"Lam, put me down," she squealed, squirming.

"You keep squirming and we'll both go down." But he was smiling.

She stopped squirming, laughing a little.

"He's got you, Momma." Jilly giggled.

"Cowboy-Man strong," Amy added.

Lam didn't say a word, not when her fingers slid into his hair at the nape of his neck or when she rested her head against his shoulder. He kept on walking and kept the girls talking. When the porch light was within sight, Gwen told the girls to run on inside—Jax leading the way.

"Lam." It was a whisper. "You need to let me talk."

"You don't owe me an explanation." He couldn't bear to hear it.

"What did Tabby tell you?"

"You've got a television show." He cleared his throat. "That's amazing, Gwen, really amazing. With your talent, you should go on to bigger and better things. Congratulations."

"Put me down." She pushed against his chest. "Now."

He stopped, a few steps shy of the porch. "You need to rest your feet."

"You need to let me talk." She sighed, placing a hand on his chest. "First, I talked to Dominic today."

Lam froze. "You did?" He couldn't breathe.

"I had to. It was hanging over me and I…didn't want to give him that power. Not anymore." She blew out a breath. "He wanted to know where his family cookbook was, Lam. All of his family recipes—you know, something he valued." She shook her head. "Nothing about the girls. Or visiting them. Or…anything. Just a cookbook."

"I'm sorry," he murmured. What the hell was wrong with the man? Didn't he realize what a gift his family was?

How wonderful they were? If he had a choice, he'd never give them up. There was no denying the man was a rat bastard, but this had to hurt.

"I'm not. Not in the least." She pushed against him. "Put me down."

He did. But he couldn't let her go, keeping his arms loose around her. "Still, I'm proud of you—for calling him." He cleared his throat. "You're an incredible woman, Gwen."

She made an odd little grumble, almost impatient. "Second, and far more important, so you need to listen closely to this…what on earth makes you think I'd want a television show, Lambert Draeger?"

He stared at her. "You don't want to be here."

"You know this?" she asked. "Who said so?"

"It's no secret you wanted out of Last Stand as soon as possible. You wanted to travel, with your dad."

"I did. When I was young and silly. When I didn't know what mattered or what real happiness felt like. Now I do." She nodded, cradling his face in her hands. "Then I came back. And now I can't imagine leaving. There is no place bigger and better on this earth. And if you'd listen to me, you'd know *you* are the reason why." She pushed against his chest again. "You. I love you. Whether or not you love me, too, it doesn't even matter."

"Are you serious?" He pulled the ring from his pocket. "I had plans, Gwen. Amazing, romantic plans. And then you were leaving, and I wasn't going to stand in your way."

"But I'm not leaving." She touched his cheek. "I'm not."

He kissed her softly, and kept kissing her until his fear subsided. Then he could breathe again. "Good." His hands cupped her face. "Good." He kissed her temple. "You and the girls are my family."

"And you love me?" It was a whisper and a plea.

"I love you." He rested his forehead against hers. "So much, I wasn't sure I was going to survive you leaving me."

She shook her head. "Never. We're not going anywhere. We are home. With you."

"Momma?" Jilly called from the back door. "Coming?"

"Where is Momma?" Amy asked. "'s dark Momma."

"I've got her. Hold on a minute. Cowboy-Man is asking your momma to marry him," he called back. "We'll be right there." He dropped to one knee. "Will you? Marry me, Gwen?"

"Yes." She tugged him up as soon as he'd slipped the ring on her finger. "Yes."

He kissed her. "Something tells me we're going to have a theme wedding." He kissed her again.

"Oh?" she asked, between kisses.

"Fairies? Fairy princesses." He kissed her again. "Maybe even fairy princess cowgirls—that's my pick."

She laughed. "I don't care, as long as you're mine when the preacher says 'I do.'"

He swung her back up and into his arms. "You don't need to worry about that. I already am."

Epilogue

G WEN STARED AT the man waiting for her at the altar. Her girls led the way, decked out in fluffy pink tutu dresses and sparkly gem-encrusted pink cowboy boots. And, yes, wings. Even poor Jax, who was sporting a pillow with the rings, had a pair of wings.

That dog's devotion to her daughters was staggering. And heartwarming.

"You ready?" her mother asked, hooking her arm.

"More than ready."

She didn't remember getting down the aisle. The sea of faces in the audience was a blur. All that mattered was the smile on Lam's face. And what a smile.

When he took her hand in his, she held tight.

The ceremony was short, but not so short that Jax didn't almost manage to chew through the harness holding the ring pillow and wings on.

When it was all said and done, Lam hadn't just vowed to honor, love, and protect her, but he'd sworn the same to the girls.

"You may now kiss the bride," the pastor announced.

"Behave," she whispered as Lam leaned down to press a kiss to her lips. She was almost disappointed at how well he behaved.

"Me, too?" Jilly asked, reaching up for him.

"Me, too too?" Amy held her little hands together, smiling from ear to ear.

"Definitely." He scooped them up, one in each arm, and pressed a kiss to their cheeks. "You're my girls." His gaze met hers. "All three of you."

They made the trip to their barn reception in a horse-drawn carriage—because Amy and Jilly had assured them she needed one, since she was a fairy princess bride. Lam agreed. He'd pretty much agreed to everything the girls suggested, which made Gwen realize how wedding budgets quickly became ridiculous.

Still, seeing all the people she loved most so happy made it all worth it.

"It's time for another dance, Mrs. Draeger?" Lam held his hand out to her.

"Momma," Jilly whispered.

Gwen stopped.

"Cowboy-Man not grumpy," Amy said, pointing up at Lam.

"No way, Pumpkin Pie." Lam knelt in front of the girls. "Today makes us a family."

Gwen's eyes stung with happy tears. Her heart already knew that to be true, but now the rest of the world knew, too. And there was something powerful about that. Powerful and comforting.

Amy and Jilly exchanged a look.

"I tol' you," Jilly said, clapping her hands.

Amy nodded.

"What, Jilly?" Gwen asked.

"He's our daddy now." Jilly was ecstatic.

"Is he?" Amy asked.

"Do you want me to be?" It was hard for him, Gwen could tell. But he loved them as if they were his own. He always would.

Amy and Jilly nodded, smiling.

"Yes!" Amy said, hugging him.

"Yes yes yes." Jilly was hugging him too. "You are Daddy."

"I am, Jilly. I am."

"Gonna tell Gramma and Ade-Lady," Jilly said, running across the dance floor.

"Tell Jax." Amy scampered across the dance floor and sat by Jax.

"He seems to be listening to every word she says." Lam was watching Amy and Jax, a smile on his face.

"You're okay with the new name?" she asked as he led her onto the dance floor. "They would have been content to keep calling you Cowboy-Man."

He shook his head, those blue eyes locking with hers. "I don't ever want them content. I want them happy. As happy as I am that you are my wife. As happy as I am that we're a family."

She couldn't stop a tear from slipping down her cheek. "That happy?"

"I know, it's a tall order." He kissed her. "But our girls deserve it. If you're good with it, I'd like to look into making them mine legally?"

She was nodding, close to tears. "You're amazing, you know that?" Amazing and handsome and kind and hers.

"You said you've felt lucky since the girls and I came into your life, but it's the other way around, Lam. I'm the lucky one, lucky to have you."

"You have me all right." He grinned. "And now, you're stuck with me."

She slid her fingers through the hair at the nape of his neck. "I'm okay with that. Cowboy-Man." Before he kissed her, she whispered, "More than okay."

The End

If you enjoyed this book, please leave a review at your favorite online retailer! Even if it's just a sentence or two it makes all the difference.

Thanks for reading *Sweet on the Cowboy* by Sasha Summers!

Discover your next romance at TulePublishing.com.

TULE
PUBLISHING

If you enjoyed *Sweet on the Cowboy,*
you'll love the next book in….

The Draegers of Last Stand, Texas series

Book 1: *Sweet on the Cowboy*

Book 2

Available now at your favorite online retailer!

About the Author

Sasha Summers grew up surrounded by books. Her passions have always been storytelling, romance and travel—passions she's used to write more than 20 romance novels and novellas. Now a best-selling and award winning-author, Sasha continues to fall a little in love with each hero she writes.

From easy-on-the-eyes cowboy, sexy alpha-male werewolves, to heroes of truly mythic proportions, she believes that everyone should have their happy ending—in fiction and real life.

Sasha lives in the suburbs of the Texas Hill country with her amazing and supportive family and her beloved grumpy cat, Gerard, The Feline Overlord. She looks forward to hearing from fans and hopes you'll visit her online at sashasummers.com.

Thank you for reading

Sweet on the Cowboy

If you enjoyed this book, you can find more from all our great authors at TulePublishing.com, or from your favorite online retailer.

TULE
PUBLISHING

CPSIA information can be obtained
at www.ICGtesting.com
Printed in the USA
LVHW090815130820
663046LV00007B/2014